# DO THE WEIRD CRIME, SERVE THE WEIRD TIME

A man who terrifies women for fun, a would-be mystery writer stalking his unscrupulous editors, an old man fantasizing about shooting his neighbor, Brittany Spears revenging her kidnapping, a wannabe writer actually killing people to work out his plots, madness uniting painters and critics together in a bloodbath, a magical ring revealing a hidden killer, a vampire disguised as the syringe of an old junkie, young communists developing "lucid dreaming" as an antidote to the class struggle....

The stranger the crime, the stranger the punishment, in this happy marriage of crime writing, horror, and surrealism. Lance Olsen writes: "Don Webb's world makes Julio Cortázar's look a little predictable, Philip K. Dick's a drab shade of mimetic."

We live in a weirder and weirder world, no doubt about it—and Don Webb is the writer riding the crest of that wave. Cutting-edge tales from inside the curl.

Borgo Press Books by DON WEBB

*Do the Weird Crime, Serve the Weird Time: Tales of
   the Bizarre*
*The War with the Belatrin*
*Webb's Weird Wild West: Western Tales of Horror*

# DO THE WEIRD CRIME, SERVE THE WEIRD TIME

## TALES OF THE BIZARRE

## DON WEBB

THE BORGO PRESS

MMXI

DO THE WEIRD CRIME, SERVE THE WEIRD TIME

FIRST EDITION

Published by Wildside Press LLC

www.wildsidebooks.com

# DEDICATION

**In memory of the world's
best weird crime writer,
William S. Burroughs**

# CONTENTS

# ACKNOWLEDGMENTS

THESE STORIES WERE previously published as follows, and are reprinted (with minor editing, updating, and textual modifications) by permission of the author:

"The Divorce" was first published in *Fear* #3 (November/December 1988). Copyright © 1988, 2011 by Don Webb.

"Shrimp Anarchy" was first published in *Fringeware Review* #9 (1995), and republished in *Serve it Forth: Cooking with Anne McCaffrey* (1996). Copyright © 1995, 1996, 2011 by Don Webb.

"The Game" was first published in *Bone Chilling Tales* #1 (1990). Copyright © 1990, 2011 by Don Webb.

"Ring of the Red Knight" was first published in *Talebones* #8, Summer 1997, and has been expanded for this book. Copyright © 1997, 2011 by Don Webb.

"The Ice Palace," "Yoga for Bolsheviks," "What Are Best Friends For?", "The Syringe," "My Heart Shifting as Sand," "The Joy of Cola," "Our Novel," "Diary Found in an Abandoned Studio," and "The Thirtyers" are published here for the first time. Copyright © 2011 by Don Webb.

# THE DIVORCE

It was to be their last fiction together. They'd had five years of various fictions depending more on courtesy and self-image than passion. The first fiction—or at least the first formally agreed to—was the Open Marriage. (It was his idea, but authorship of ideas was never mentioned—they did everything together, the second fiction.) He had thought it was for him alone, a need based on misapprehended biology. She counted his infidelities as crimes, but quietly to herself. Her only remedy, as they say judicially, were her own infidelities. This last fiction, the Friendly Divorce, was also his idea, but came closer to collaboration than any of the others.

Everything would become "final" next Monday. Both had cars, incomes and apartments. Only money was left to be divided. In the spirit of a true rite of passage they decided to blow it all in Vegas. They went to the bank on Monday, the Monday a week before "Final" Monday, and turned everything into cash. They carefully and oh so scrupulously pushed it into two piles. On Wednesday they left. On the road they'd outdone each other in kindnesses—paying for gas, for picture postcards, for dinner and drinks. Both figured they'd lose their shares in Vegas. Going back to GO, starting a new game. They'd been penniless to start and a return to that status would somehow erase the intervening five years.

On Thursday morning they'd hit the desert and conversation had dried up. In the quiet air-conditioned hiss of "his" Wagoneer remarks of the last few months echoed. She was from the "shallow end of the gene-pool." He was as "tenderhearted as a coprolite." The *mot juste* being another example of their common artistry.

Midmorning she spotted a sign, "Roy's Rockshop and Restaurant." It promised slot machines, poisonous reptiles, rare desert rocks, cactus candy, and a bottomless coffee cup. The coffee sounded good. The other could provide conversational fodder until they reached Vegas. Five miles later she pulled in. The rockshop had two concrete teepees out front, no doubt the dwelling place of the tribe that makes the rubber tomahawks for souvenirs. It was further adorned with four cow skulls with outdoor Christmas lights for eyes.

When they went in the white-haired proprietor had snapped awake. The owner started the coffee, apologized for the lack of poisonous reptiles—some young kids stole all the cages last year—and discussed local politics.

He ordered the Eye Opener: two poached eggs (underdone), orange juice (frozen), whole wheat toast, jelly. She ordered the Rancho Deluxe: scrambled eggs with salsa, biscuits (stale), jelly, bottomless cup of coffee. They sat on green vinyl-covered revolving bar stools, which had they been of an earlier generation would have called up romantic visions of drugstore dating. The owner asked where they was from? Lubbock, Texas. This led to a discussion of his niece who'd went to Texas Tech. They didn't teach at the University, did they? No. Well they probably wouldn't know her? Afraid not. Where are you going? Vegas to gamble a little and have fun.

The proprietor reckoned that not many people go through the desert to see its natural beauty. This reckoning lasted three coffee cups. An ancient black Chevy pickup pulled up. An equally ancient-looking Navajo came in. The proprietor poured him a cup of coffee. The proprietor introduced the Indian as Tonky. During the next two cups of coffee the owner told Tonky all about them. She wanted the check. Tonky was silent. He had left his yolk-covered plate and wandered over to look at the dusty bins of geodes and quartz crystal clusters.

She finally got the check. When she paid, Tonky asked her if they was going to Vegas? She said yes.

Her husband walked up carrying an amethyst-filled geode from Brazil. Tonky explained a shortcut. She didn't really understand it, but decided not to ask for clarification. For one thing, her soon-to-be-ex-husband had always thought her small-brained. For another his body language screamed impatience.

He bought the purple geode and gave it to her. She

said it was treasure. The proprietor said it was sweet to see married people so much in love. Tonky walked around the counter to pour himself another cup of coffee. They left.

The short cut began—as best she understood—at a two-lane road leaving the highway after a mile and a half. When the two-lane did appear, she decided she had understood Tonky's muddled directions after all. As she turned off the road she watched for his reaction, but he just stared into the violet depths of the geode.

Sixteen miles later she decided she was lost. Reluctantly she admitted it. He told her to turn around. There was a dirt road about two miles back that should intersect the highway. He'd been waiting for this. Preparing to show her up.

The dirt road was noisy and small. She hoped she wouldn't meet any oncoming traffic. He smiled and said it didn't look like there'd been any traffic at all for a long time.

A tiny wooden bridge over a fairly steep arroyo broke as the Wagoneer crossed it going sixty m.p.h. She remembered being airborne for a minute.

When she came to she was sitting upside down hanging by the seatbelt harness. The windshield was a spider web around a wall of sandstone and gypsum. Blood was running up her face through her hair and onto the ceiling below. He was moaning. He wasn't in the car.

Getting down from the harness was easy after she realized that she could fall sideways against the half-open door. The door opened completely and she fell onto the hot red sand. It took a long time to stand up. Her bleeding seemed to have stopped.

He was lying about two car lengths away. His face was red. He was moaning quietly. She ran over. He reached up she caught his arm. He gasped.

Then he was quiet. Not moving. Not breathing.

She started to release his hand. Then stopped herself. What if she couldn't let go? She'd been trying to let go for five years. What if she failed this time? What a crazy thought—the blood loss must be making her crazy. She laughed. Laughing hurt. She drug his body over to the shade of the overturned Wagoneer. She decided to hold on a while, it was only right. You couldn't just leave someone so—suddenly.

She had to figure out what to do. She couldn't carry him to the freeway. She didn't know which way was quicker. She squeezed the dead hand as though he would wake up and tell her. Maybe he was right after all. After a long time, after the flies came, she decided what to do.

\* \* \* \* \* \* \*

The Highway Patrol picked her up. It wasn't just her bloody face or agitated manner. It was the severed hand she carried.

# THE ICE PALACE

The widow MacPhearson never did anything. She was just like me, she never went out at night, never talked on the hone. Nothing.

She wasn't doing anything the night of the Fourth, the night she was shot. I wanted to know. I wanted to know exactly what kind of nothing she was doing that night. She and I are the same age, excepting now of course she is dead, actually if she were alive she would have been six months older than me, which doesn't matter much now, but kept us in separate grades in school.

I was retired, but she kept working. I had worked the Sears catalog show room. Doublesign, Texas had had the last Sears catalog showroom in the country. It should have been closed years ago, but a clerical error kept it going. I am fascinated by errors. Maybe the people that shot her, had meant to shoot me. Maybe they just had the wrong address. A simple computer error. I hate computers. I had to stop working just as computers came in.

Velma MacPhearson also had no truck with computers. She ran the Ice Palace, which was a place to buy soft ice cream and shakes near the state park. There weren't many places like that left. I mean not affiliated with some big chainlike Dairy Queen. When she was working there years ago, everyone called the Ice Queen, because she had no truck with men either. She wasn't rude to us, just a little cold, just like ice cream. But as she got old no one would have wanted her anyway, so we stopped calling her the Ice Queen. I have heard her called the Ice Bitch, but I was brought up never to call a lady things like that (even if they were true).

I wish she hadn't been so cold to men. She would have made a good neighbor. Both of us were in bad health. Hers was worse though. She was past the time in life when you should have to stand and make a living. I think she had enough money to retire, just no one to give her permission to do so.

The sheriff said the FBI came into town after her killing. She was killed by a serial killer. I don't know what he killed or why. Maybe it was just women that worked in the ice cream industry. Maybe just people that were Ice Bitches. I want to know.

I was at the VFW hall. I had lied about my age to get into the end of WWII. That was how my legs wound up the way they are. Which is another reason I wanted a nice neighbor. My kids pulled a mean trick on me. They both died, so that I am alone a good deal.

I know she used to watch TV, because I could hear it. I could have heard the shot, except I was at the VFW hall. We were watching the fireworks show. Last

Fourth of July of the century, of the millennium. I had to listen to idiots explaining Y2K to other idiots, but it was people. I have always needed people.

People will tell you who you are.

One of my big fears is that I won't have any people around me when it is time to pull the plug. I could fall and they could put me into one of those damn life support machines, and I could live forever.

Someone came to pull Velma's plug.

They just walked in off the street.

I can't believe that. I can't believe that someone could just kill you without even knowing you. There must be a mistake. Maybe it was somebody that she shorted for change. She did that. I've seen her cheat a tourist out of a dime or a nickel, a quarter if she was feeling bold. They lost their quarter and they came to get her. I could live with that. It puts a price tag on human life.

She was in her bedroom on the second floor. Ever since that night I have slept in my second floor bedroom. She and her runaway husband had bought their house, but I inherited mine. In the "historic" center of downtown Doublesign. That's because it has the old library and the post office and places for people to sell junktiques to tourists. Otherwise it would be just plain old. It isn't very likely that you'll meet anyone that lives in the house they were born in, but I do. I will die here.

I have been sleeping in the second floor, because all I can do is think about her death.

She was shot twice. Once by a .22 at close range and once by a kid's dart gun. That's how they know it was this serial killer. I wonder if they shot her with the dart gun first, or second.

Imagine if it was first. You know someone has broken into your house. They had come in through a window facing the backyard. She must have heard them come up the stairs. She probably screamed, and then *whup* she is hit with a dart. She must have been so relieved. It was all a joke, a prank, and then *blammo* a real bullet into her head making a third eye.

I saw her when they took her away. I wanted it all from my upstairs window. Then the sheriff came to talk me about it. I had been down at the VFW Hall listening to a recorded version of Elvis signing "Dixie." So mainly he told me about it, rather than me answering his questions. He called her "the Ice Bitch."

I don't know what is wrong with ice. Many of my friends have moved out of Texas because they can't take the heat. They are living with their kids in some cool town. Those that live here, spend all their time inside, with their air conditioners turned up so far that if they were to die, their body wouldn't be in any danger of rotting. It seems a safer way to die.

I bet her body was very cool, when they carried it out.

I can't get this place very cool. It's those damn high ceilings. You see they used to build ceilings very, very high to encourage circulation of air. This was a cool house in my grandfather's time. But I can run my AC all the time and It doesn't get cool. I think about cool things when I am going to sleep. I think of icy mountain springs, and snow and ice cream. I think about the soft ice cream down at the Ice Palace. Before I got diabetes, I used to dream of just sticking my mouth under the spigot and letting the thick stream of soft ice cream fill me up, make me good and cool.

I always envied her her job at the Ice Palace. I used to work in a catalog showroom. That meant mainly I helped people look things up in a catalog and then order them. That what webpages do now. Sometimes people were happy when they used my service. They were ordering swing sets for the children or luggage for a round-the-world trip. But sometimes they were unhappy. They ordered home repairs, or equipment that let them use the tub safely and so forth. But I was never there when they would get their stuff. I never got to see the real smile—the smile of ownership—of material culture. All I got was vague smiles of hope. This was something that Mrs. MacPhearson had over all of us. Everyone is happy to buy ice cream. Even the little kids she used to be mean to, were still happy to buy ice cream. I don't think you can look at an ice cream cone and be unhappy.

I have seen many unhappy people.

Constance, my wife, was unhappy. I saw her unhappy face for many years, and everything I did, everything I tried, made her more unhappy. She died young, escaping me the way Velma's husband did her. Of course he didn't die. He just bought the Ice Palace and then ran off and left her to pay for it for many years. It wasn't the Ice Palace to start with it, it was the

Golden Bucket and sold chicken. It never did well, but the Ice Palace did OK. It even did OK enough for her to have one or two young girls work there with her in the summer. It didn't do crap in the winter, but she would be down there. I have driven by when there was snow on the ground and seen the widow's unhappy face, just staring at the snow. She would be open all day for that one cup of coffee she would sell. But she didn't have anything else. All she had was the Ice Palace. She lived across the street from the library and didn't go. She didn't even allow herself cable TV. Up every morning to wash it up, and then serve the pre-lunch crowd of farmers that came in to drink coffee, and once-in-a-great-while have a single ice cream cone. Then lunch. Local people. The afternoons filled with tourists back from the state park. Small dinner trade, then the local kids out riding around. Everyday she knew what she had to do.

I don't know what I have to do. I don't wake up in the morning with a plan. Someday I go to the barber, some days I cut my grass. I take some of the old men, who are worse off than me, to the doctor. I get my car serviced. Time flies by. It seems like every week, I'm getting my car serviced. My life was never as full as the widow MacPhearson's. Maybe that was why they shot her. Maybe she had used her share of life's resources. Maybe there's only so many new faces you get to see, so many people that you talk to. Then some agency in the world intervenes. But probably not with a.22, probably such cosmic allotments are determined by angels.

I don't know about angels. I have never been sure about God. I've thought I should drag my butt down to church, so I would get a chance to meet people, talk with people. I think it has been ten years since anyone stepped into my house. I mean other than a plumber.

I wonder if Velma thought about God, when they shot her.

She knew she was going to be shot that's the important part. She had been sitting at the swivel chair at her desk in the bedroom. She would have swiveled argon as they came up the stairs. They had clipped off her power. Things were dark. I bet she was getting up the steam to go downstairs and check her fuse box. Her wiring was bad, like every house on this block, they hadn't figured on people having washing machines and dishwashers and satellite TV. She probably had already turned around, with that very resolved and determined face she had for everything, and was about to get up. She would have seen them head first. She would have known if she knew them.

If the FBI is right, she would have known that she didn't know them. So she had to know she was going to die. People don't show up in the dark to give you flowers.

She could have seen the cold barrel of the gun. The light from the street light would have let her see it. I have measured this. My own bedroom is just as far from the streetlight. I have tried to make it just like hers. I turnoff all the lights and then I try out different things with mirrors and stopwatches. I want to know how long she had to think about it. She couldn't have time to think all the things I've thought about it. I've had weeks and weeks. I suspect that she had less than a minute, from when she saw them to the bullet entering her forehead.

She didn't get up. She was sitting when the bullet struck. Maybe she was really defiant, refusing to get up for some hooligan that had disturbed her house. Maybe she was afraid. I've got to know what she thought. That way I'm prepared. I can't imagine an event like that happening. How can you die and not be prepared? So I try out things.

I got the key to her house.

No one knows this. I did not tell the sheriff. Long ago she gave a key to my wife, so that my wife could carry in the mail and newspaper; when Velma had to go to Ohio that time and take care of her sister. My wife never gave the key back.

I remembered it a few days after the shooting. The FBI had come and gone and the sheriff was done with the place. There would be some months before the county would figure out who the house belonged to. So it just set there full of darkness and mystery.

One night I waited till two in the morning and then I went in. I took a little flashlight and made my way up the stairs. I went to her swivel chair and I sat down in it, swiveling around each time the hose settled, trying to imagine the killer coming up the stairs in the dark. I could see his head; it was almost like he was there, but I didn't know what I would think. What would my last thoughts be, if I knew they would be my last thoughts. I wondered if she would have thought of her husband that had abandoned her forty years ago.

Just think of it. She was with that guy for six, seven months and that was what had shaped her whole life. It gave her the Ice Palace. It gave her a reputation as a woman that men run away from. It gave her every unhappy day. All the other six months, all the half years since had done so much less, except for the night of the Fourth. Perhaps it set her free.

I have been back in the house more often. At first I was very careful. I would late until early morning. Some mornings I couldn't do it. I would fall asleep about midnight, and then when I opened my eyes, rosy-fingered dawn had taken the sky. I realized though, that no could see me enter from the back of her house, anyway. Just as no one had seen the killer enter. I would just wait until nightfall.

The house was hot, since there was no power and therefore no AC. I really thought a good deal about ice cream. Someone had emptied out the refrigerator. I guess that is lagniappe for the sheriff. Since the crime investigation is over I can *touch* things. I touch her desk, I lay in her bed. Sometimes I get down on all fours and touch the bloodstain on the carpet with my forehead. I listen. Thing are very quiet in the house, so you can hear anything. I heard a leaf from one of her big maples hit the roof. In a few months it will be autumn. Soon the house will belong to somebody. Maybe the county can claim it, but it will stop being empty. Stop being our house.

I wish she could tell me what she thought.

I tried to find out things from the sheriff about the investigation, but he either knew nothing, or told me nothing. I found out that he talked about me. There's a bar in town called the Shamrock, and I went there the night in August when it had been over a hundred that day and I needed something cool. I hadn't been in years, and the bartender told me that the sheriff said I was obsessed about the case. Implied I was in love with the widow MacPhearson.I laughed. He laughed. I ain't never going in there again.

I'm not in love with her. I just want to know what she thought. I lived next to her for forty years. I don't know what she thought.

We were both the same. We never took vacations. We we're born here. We never left the city except briefly. We looked out at the same street. We knew the same people. We read *Reader's Digest* and the *TV Guide*. We shopped at the Sac-n-Pac and the HEB. Watered our lawns on the same days. Everyday she would say to me, "Good Evening Mr. Clemens." Most of the year, she would add, "Hot enough for you?" I would say "Good Evening Mrs. MacPhearson, can't complain and it wouldn't do any good if I did." I never asked her what would happen if suddenly some were to kill her. Kill her with a real bullet and then bounce a dart off of her. I never asked what she would be thinking of. Suddenly it was dark, darker than it had been for forty years since her husband ran out on her, dark. She would be assessing whether or not to bother to try and fix the lights, and habit and "common sense" would say, "yes, go fix the lights." Then she would hear the killer's footsteps. Come at last, after all those years of waiting. She may have had time to straighten her hair. Time to formulate one last greeting. No, she would have been silent. Silent like I am every night as I sit in her chair. She would have turned to face them. She had forty years to prepare. Up till the last minute, she would have thought that it could have been him, coming back after all those years to thank her for keeping their dream alive after so many miserable lonely mornings. Thank you, honey. And she could have told him— what? Which of the many speeches prepared for over the years.

But it wasn't him. Just some random person, like any of the faces that she saw in the Ice Palace everyday. Then she had a moment for her last thought on earth.

I pray every night when I sit here, that her last thought was of ice cream, thick and flowing from the spigot, flowing on into eternity.

# SHRIMP ANARCHY

1½ cup onion
1 cup celery
2 medium green peppers
4 cloves garlic
1 lb. cleaned raw shrimp
¼ cup margarine
2 cups tomato sauce
1 cup water
2 tsps. minced parsley
1 tsp. salt
1 tsp. Cayenne pepper
2 bay leaves
3 cups rice (prepare separately)

Chop onion, celery, peppers, and garlic. Cook in margarine fat for about five minutes. Remove from heat; stir in tomato sauce, water and seasonings. Simmer about ten minutes. Add shrimp, cover and cook for ten to twenty minutes until shrimp are pink and tender. Serve over hot rice.

While shrimp are in preparation have your local troop perform the following actions:

I. Begin calling all local branches of the federal government and tell them that their department has come under fire in the national budget cutting process. Advise them that the only hope for their jobs is an immediate flight to Washington to testify before the Senate finance committee. The bureaucrats will then flee their offices. As they abandon their offices, send paint crews to rename the offices for plumbing and artistic firms. Change locks. The resulting confusion will end federal control of your area.

II. Blow up all cable TV facilities in your area. Call all local TV stations. Threaten them with destruction unless they agree to show nothing but the "What Makes Auntie Freeze?" episode of *My Mother the Car*. This will cause all but the most brain damaged among the local populace to turn off their sets and begin to think. For those who still remain addicted to the tube, there isn't any hope anyway.

III. Call up all the local schools, identifying yourselves as the local fire Marshall, tell them it is time for an impromptu fire drill. Call up all firms which provide ice cream refreshments from trucks. Tell the trucks to head to the schools, that a special school holiday has just been declared and the kids will want to celebrate. Remind them to announce the holiday over their loud speakers as the they approach the schools.

IV. Call the local churches, synagogues and mosques. Tell them that the largest churches in the city have started a raffle program that gives money to a random church goer. Ask them if they have a statement on the how much money **They would pay** to have someone to attend their church. Tell them that all the other churches are making statements at the local radio stations. Call all the local radio stations and tell them that church groups are making a hostile march on them *en masse*. Tell the radio stations the only way to avoid religious attack is to quickly found their own religions and start broadcasting them right away. Tell them that the churches won't attack their own. This will cause the state's greatest ally in enslavement, the churches, and the state's second greatest ally, the media to fight amongst themselves.

V. Call up local government offices and tell them that the feds are planning to absorb all their functions in a few days. Say that the governor/mayor has said that the only way folks may keep their jobs is if they picket all federal buildings, with placards marked "Power to the People!". The federals will have all left, and the arriving picketers will be picketing the locksmiths and painting crews. Call the local newspapers and ask them why all our local government is downtown picketing honest working men and women? Why is local government opposed to Labor? Express a hope that the local newspaper will cover the story, since all the radio seems to talk about any more is religion.

VI. Call the police and announce that the biggest shopping mall in town is offering a free fifty dollar gift certificate to the first two hundred police men who show up in uniform at the mall. Call all the malls and tell them that the police are in a state of revolt, and are coming to mall after mall to loot freely. If they doubt the story call up the biggest mall and ask if the police are coming in number. Tell them that to avoid panic, they should leave the malls—keeping all the doors open and hope that the police will take what they want and just go away. Tell to the homeless in your neighborhoods, that it's a good day to visit the malls for a clothing upgrade.

VII. At this point shrimp will be done, go home, eat shrimp, start next batch.

VIII. Go to all the empty churches, synagogues, and mosques. Put large hand lettered signs on each. "Going out of Business sale! All furniture free for hauling." Give everyone that shows up some of those anarchists zines,you've been storing for years. Numerous copies of *The Stars My Destination* are also nice gifts. Help people loot the churches, synagogues, and mosques. Tell each one of them, "Well we're going to have start figuring this stuff out for ourselves now." Mention that all the local government offices have gone out of business too, and that everything there's free as well.

IX. Get a large electromagnetic crane, such as the kind used in car demolition lots. Use its mighty magnetic field to wipe away all records at banks, courthouses, and taxation offices.

X. Storm the electric power station. Turn all power of in the city for twenty three minutes.

XI. In the instability that will follow use your judgment and creativity to change a mindless falling away of the system into an individualistic small scale society unlike any that have existed in history save for our dreams. Some ice-cream would be nice too, since the shrimp burns a little. Maybe served with out anarchy. Serves four.

# THE GAME

In all other respects he is a benevolent conformist. He decided that all men are allowed one vice. Open or hidden. The best vices—although, he would admit that one doesn't rationally choose one's vices—the best vices are the ones that do not destroy the practitioner or permanently injure his victim. Although he gave little thought to his victims. He dealt in fear. He stalked women. He never did anything to his victims. He never even caught them. Or attempted to do these things. Or thought of these things.

Anytime can be a beginning. He would sit on a bench in a park (or an airport, or a shopping mall) and wait. Something would catch his eye. A startling silhouette or a dress ablaze with purple. Then he would rise—quietly, discreetly. He would follow the woman. Never women or a woman with a man or men. Such things could lead to consequences that could disturb his real life. His eight-to-five job forty-nine weeks a year. He relished the backward glance. He could detect the whole continuum: notice, curiosity, confirmation, alarum, fear, flight. The women didn't cry out to security guards or passersby. He never pressed that close. If she paused to study mannequins, he paused to review the wares of B. Dalton. If she stopped for a drink in a fountain, he would admire the maidenhair tree. If she ran, he would return to his bench. Never, never run in public. The woman would go to her car, he to his (in his college days a ten-speed racing bike sufficed). He would follow her to her house or apartment through labyrinthine suburbs and careful turning tricks. The more elusive she was the greater his excitement. He can't stand it when some great event occurs and interferes with his ploys.

Today, this brilliant Friday, seemed as good a day as any. Summer chases could be very long as wily women led him into the twilight. He sat on a boulder in a pocket park in LaGrange Park. He waited. It had been a busy day bristling with office politics, vague corporate depravities, and hour-long calls to Japan. All of this tension slid from his back into the gray slate. He was ready. He spotted a young woman feeding pigeons. She looked intelligent, enough. Hope she doesn't live here. She looked up and smiled. He smiled. She glanced up from time to time. Each time she caught his eye. Nervousness began. She quick walked to her car—a red BMW a sign of upward mobility and great resourcefulness. Good.

He went to his baby blue Continental—slightly revved up—slightly improved. A man has to spend money on his secret vice. That's how you measure his devotion to it.

To his glee, she quickly left LaGrange Park heading

northward for the lake. She might even be from out of town. Illinois plates. Soon they were on the Miracle Mile.

Traffic was very dense today. Soon everything came to a standstill. Something had gone wrong. Her car was two cars ahead. He could see her watch him in her mirror. This wasn't how the game was played. It wasn't any fun anymore.

He resolved that when things started up again he'd just drive straight home. Unless she followed him. No that was unthinkable. People began turning off their motors. He checked his tank—one quarter full. With the modifications the LTD consumed great quantities of gas. He turned off his car missing the air conditioning instantly. Windows went down everywhere. Not his. When he played the game he liked to feel cut off. Remote. Frankly he felt dirty. There's a lot of dirt in a solitary vice, a vice that no one else even thinks of—let alone practices.

People began to talk. No doubt filling the silence with the cheap inventiveness of the bored commuter. He could hear the waves of the lake. It had been a long time since he had heard them. How long? Memory seemed uncertain. He was losing touch. Too much detritus from the gray world of the office. How could you tell Monday from Wednesday, or March from May? How could you tell what happened in which May or how many Mays had gone by? He needed real experiences. He would do the things he'd done as a child. He would begin as soon as this traffic jam was over.

No boats on the lake today. Some people, some irresponsible people had begun to leave their cars. How would these vehicles ever get moving if some of them were abandoned—blocking key lanes? He began to inventory his childhood experiences deciding which to re-create first.

Perhaps a noise, a siren or a gong sounded during his reverie. Everyone seemed to be leaving his or her cars. Let them. He had a good idea. When they were gone he would walk up to the young woman. Make a contact for once. A real human contact. In only seconds all the cars were empty. He walked to the BMW. It, too, was empty. He had expected her to stay, although he wasn't sure why.

Suddenly he was afraid. A child of the nuclear generation he could imagine only one disaster. He ran for the nearest building, a tall round hotel topped with a rotating restaurant. It looked like a giant child-proof bottle. The lobby was empty. No emergency instructions crackled over the PA system. He went to the elevator. He must get down. To the core of the earth. It arrived and he descended to the sub-basement. Fluorescent light showed a jungle of brightly painted pipes. Maybe it was safe here.

Where was everybody? He returned to the lobby. He shouted. Shouting did not come easily to him. He had to warm up to it with several half-shouts. Finally he achieved full volume. No one here. At least, no one answered him. He walked to his car. The radio stations were off the air, except for one FM easy-listening station that was entirely automatic.

He came back to the hotel. He borrowed a room key. TV was still going. It lasted about half an hour. He locked his room but he didn't know what he locked it against. He read *What to Do in Chicago* and the Book of Revelations. The lights flickered about nine and then went out. He was hungry. He made his way in the dark to a vending machine. He smashed the glass with a chair and picked up the display candy and peanut butter-filled crackers. He unwrapped them carefully—feeling the chocolate with his blind fingers afraid of swallowing a fragment of glass. He returned to his room, drank a lot of water, and locked his door.

The next day he ascended the fire stairs to the restaurant and ate a smoked chicken from a warming refrigerator. He watched the still city. The empty lake.

He decided he was singularly deficient of survival skills. He neither hunted nor fished. When he ran out of food—he would visit a nearby pharmacy.

The phone was dead.

He hadn't thought of it 'til now.

He returned to his room. He could steal everything. He could be the wealthiest man in the world. Tomorrow he would explore things.

He went to all the shops of the Miracle Mile—seeing all the luxuries his life had denied him.

On the third day he woke to the sounds of motors starting. He ran out of his room. People had returned.

They were silent. They avoided his eyes.

He would never, never bridge the gap.

# YOGA FOR BOLSHEVIKS

*I believe that we need an aristocracy in which each person can be an aristocrat. That is to say every human being is entitled to a legitimate pride in his environment and antecedents. The Socialist vision is somewhat similar. However it insists too much on material values. Its appeal is to those people who cannot respect themselves without good clothes and well-filled tummies. That is a wrong assumption. An Indian no matter how dire his poverty can dispense hospitality with dignity. He is his own welcome. Roger W. Babson once asked me what I thought was the solution of the high cost of living. I answered, "The Indian system. Fewer wants." He that knows he is as good a man as his neighbor does not need to impress by evidence of material wealth.*

*Professor Joe Gould*

The New Atlantis Bookstore is a small oasis from downtown Austin, full of the delicious tang of yellowing paper and an astonishingly great number of used books crammed into its shelves. It is the last of a noble line fighting for life: Paperbacks Plus, Libby's Used Books, Grok Books, Adventures in Crime and Space. The proprietor John Reynman sees the handwriting on the wall, but what kind of man derives truth from ectoplasmic graffiti?

John Reynman stood behind the counter thinking about how to tell Haidee about the day. All happily married couples give each other the gift of narration— a little story about their time apart polished with nice phrases, clever retorts and dramatic emphasis. He would sum up his current situation by saying that he had his best and his worst customers in at the same time. He sipped his coffee from a chipped white and blue coffee cup and smiled as the books piled up. It bore the phrase, "Think Big Be a Teacher Texas Teaching Fellows." He had found it on the sidewalk four years ago. John is like that. He picks things up.

Jeff Williams stacked book after book on the counter. Jeff was a thin tall man with coarse black hair and the fevered brown bloodshot eyes of a Poe. He wore black denim pants and a black t-shirt proclaiming his loyalty to the Electric Luddites. His studied casualness was ruined only by the Rolex on his wrist. His stack of hardbacks would easily run seventy bucks and he kept going back for more. John was glad to see them go; Jeff was buying every book on yoga that John had. These books moved slowly, and occult titles tended to be stolen fairly often. Porn for the soul....

John began ringing Jeff's purchases up so that he

could get him out of the store quicker.

Frank Goldman claimed to have passed the century mark the year before. His head was almost without its white hair anymore, his wrinkles had wrinkles and his eyes had *sunken* so much that he looked like a revenant from a Poe story. Frank had very little money, and had never really had any. He had been beached like a whale in Austin during the Great Depression, when his cash ran out before he could make it to the fabled land of Hollywood, California. His life had been a series of questionable deals, dicey schemes and downright frauds. He had been on the fringes of oddball politics, music promotion, and other less identifiable industries for decades—which gave him a priceless commodity of stories. He could tell you about being an extra in *Texas Chainsaw Massacre*, or sleeping with Janis Joplin, or selling counterfeit ration stamps during the Second World War. He had great drinking bouts with governors, made love to congressmen's wives, smoked dope with Willie Nelson, and been a UFO watcher for Project Starlight International. Each story that he gave from his word-horde was a spell that John could enchant his customers with for weeks. Sure Frank never paid for his books, and got many free coffees over at the Decline of the West, but nobody felt cheated. Frank had chosen one book *Civilized Shamans*, a hardback about Tibet and was shuffling forward. Jeff nearly ran him over, as he passed the old man to grab the bright yellow *Yoga for Dummies*.

"I think I got everything, Mr. Reynman." Said Jeff.

"Looks like it. If I have any more titles that have wandered off I'll let you know. I am going out to the warehouse this weekend and I'll check to see if I can find anything more." Said John. "It comes to $83.75."

Jeff pulled a crumple of money out of his jeans, a twenty escaped and hit the floor. Frank stared at it. John nodded at it and Jeff picked up the money saying "Sorry."

As John made change, Frank walked up to the counter.

"Young man, I see that you are interested in the study of yoga." Said Frank.

"I saw this *Discovery* special on it last night, and I was thinking how little time any of us are in control of our thoughts, so I thought I would change that about myself."

Frank nodded. "Yes, it was the secret of yoga that gave me my long life and all of my happiness despite the circumstances of my life."

Jeff looked at Frank's palsy, his liver spots, and his ancient eyes. Frank looked at the watch.

"You studied yoga?"

"Not in the east, but here in Austin in the Thirties from James Cassutto. He was a great Western master, who learned a mixture of Indian and Native American techniques."

"I've never heard of him" said Jeff.

"There was some *controversy* about his teachings." Said Frank playing his trump card. "I could tell you more but I need to sit a spell."

"Would you like me to buy you coffee next door?" asked Jeff. "I know the staff there very well."

"That would be very kind, but I can't stand coffee, could you get me a tea?"

Jeff scooped up his books and took the old man's hand. There was even the pretense of buying the book about Tibet. John put it on Jeff's tab. As many books as he bought he would never notice.

John Reynman ran into Jeff and Frank a couple of days later. John had help on Wednesdays and was able to take a nice long lunch at Sanna's, a downtown restaurant and tea-room, a few blocks from the New Atlantis He was midway though a tasty Cesar salad with chicken when he saw them across the crowded restaurant. Frank wore an old gray three-piece suit that swallowed his shrunken frame and Jeff was in shiny black shorts and a blue-and-white-stripped cotton shirt. Frank was making expansive gestures with his hands and Jeff was watching him like a bunny watches a rattlesnake. The check came and Jeff picked it up and dashed out of the restaurant. Frank slowly surveyed the restaurant as he made his way to the door and spotted John. He headed over and sat at John's booth.

"Watching my show were ya?" asked Frank. "Don't be afraid he'll be back in your store in a few days, I figure I can dine out for a week on him."

"Are you teaching him yoga?" asked John.

"Yoga my ass. I am selling a tall tale to him for a few meals. He comes out much the better on the deal if you ask me."

The waiter had come over and asked if John needed anything. Frank ordered a hot tea and a slice of chess pie.

"What tale are you selling him?" asked John.

"I don't guess it would hurt you to know. I know you despise him." Said Frank.

"I have no such feelings. Jeff is one of my most loyal customers."

"I'm sure that's true. But I see you there looking at him with disguised hate behind your coffee cup. Did you know you only drink your wretched coffee when you've got a customer you don't like? You're thinking about the fact that the guy is nearly thirty and his folks send him money to keep him from coming home."

"I didn't know he was that old."

"Faggots look much younger than their age. It's why I've always thought there was a gay gene. His folks sent him off to Austin to go to college and never come back. They have trouble dealing with his sexual preference up in Shamrock. His partner wasted away and that's a big deal in rural Texas. You and I don't have any trouble with that, but we have trouble with someone that can lay in a soft bed with a nice comforter when our alarms are going off at 7:00 and our heads hurt and we don't know if our checks might bounce and we have to figure how to pay for our medicine and so forth. How much does he drop in your store every month?"

John shrugged and then said, "I figure about eighty bucks a month. He's always got something he's interested in. One month he was going to write detective novels so he bought all my books on writing and a dozen classic detective novels. Another month he was going to be a fashion designer. So what is going to be now?"

"Most of us really don't get to choose what we want to be when we grow up. I didn't. My choice was to be a Hollywood star, the next Clark Gable. He doesn't know who Clark Gable was."

John nodded and then realized that at forty-eight, he had never actually seen a Clark Gable movie except clips from *Gone with the Wind* on YouTube.

The pie arrived and Frank dug in. Although he still had the gift of gab, John could see how frail he had become. His breathing was shallow and irregular; his hand shook.

Frank continued, "You know twenty, thirty years ago there were some great underground papers in this town. The *Austin Free Voice* asked me to write for them, tell them stories of being a Wobbly or romantic nonsense about the Depression. Yep, we were starving then, it was dang romantic. But I tried to get something going. I took a Left Wing agitator that I really knew named Cassutto, and said that he had learned a deep magical secret from an Indian shaman he had met in a chain gang. This old Indian had told him how to control his dreams. It was going to be the secret of communism. See at night you could be anything you wanted to be, dreams would no longer be a land without freedom of choice and absence of will. You could be the Emperor of China at night, and then you would be willing to be a hard struggling comrade during the day. The Castaneda books were coming out and Chief Gray Eagle, and I figured I could sell *Yoga for Bolsheviks* by Cassutto. Well nobody snapped at my little hoax then, but I'm selling it to wonder boy these days."

Frank had a coughing fit. John waited till it was done, and then asked," Are you OK? Should I help you home?"

Frank looked really angry, and shook his head no, but said, "Yes. That might not be a bad idea."

John helped him up. The old man leaned heavily on John's arm. He lived in a small apartment over a shop that sold cell phones. Frank had told him that he had lived there since 1950 "outlasting fourteen businesses." John had to pause at every step.

"You got any family?" John asked..

"Buried 'em. Buried my youngest sister ten years ago. I've got some nephews, but I don't how to get hold of them, and I'm sure they don't want to get hold of me. I just get by being a son of a bitch."

They reached the top of the stairs. Frank said, "Thank you for helping me home. I hate to be a burden to anyone." He began fumbling for his keys. His palsy was worse than at the restaurant. John said, "I need to come in and use your facilities."

"No you don't. You just want to be sure that I don't die here on the steps. Well that's probably a good thing. I talked the landlord into giving me free rent fifteen years ago. I am an Austin institution like Leslie Cochran. The sucker that would be my last year. I want to keep annoying him for awhile."

The apartment had a slanted ceiling and smelled like an old people's home. The floor's yellowish linoleum was worn through in a couple of places showing grime-blackened wood beneath. There was a bed with sheets that had not been washed in awhile with an army blanket on top of it. A roll-top desk was the single nice piece of furniture in the room contrasting with the two broken down orange plastic chairs clearly salvaged from some alley. A small nightstand had a hot plate on it with a rather disreputable looking copper teapot.. There was an open bottle of Benchmark bourbon and case of assorted can goods set next to the nightstand. Mixed veggies and Fancy Feast—so people really do eat cat food. Cheap overstuffed bookshelves covered the walls. There was no TV, no radio, and no phone. John went into the small bathroom, and closed the door behind him. The fifteen-watt bulb didn't give much light, and given the filth inside John was glad of that. He heard Frank sit on the bed. He flushed and went back to the main room.

Frank said, "You can see that I don't entertain much anymore." He waved a shaky hand around the room. "Are you disappointed? Expected a pleasure palace after all of my stories?"

"I think wherever you live is a good place because it has a grand old man there." said John.

"Oh Jesus save the mark!" said Frank. "I outlived everything and everybody. That's why I can't stand our young friend. He'll miss all of his connections too.

I am going to cure him of dreaming."

"Did someone ever cure you of dreaming?" asked John.

"No. Dreaming's all I got. At night I'm the emperor of China." Frank stood up. His color grew paler and his steps were unsteady. He walked over to the roll top desk. He started to open it, and then said, "You're a good man John. I think you're good enough. I thought that when you let run-always live in your little shop and work the counter. You didn't know I knew that, did you?"

"I try to keep it a secret so the shop won't attract the wrong kind of people. One a year or so is all that Haidee and I can afford."

"See? You are a good man. I wasn't good enough, but I'm not bad man. I did one good thing in my life. I always kept 'em guessing—that's the best thing you can do if you want to be a very old man." Frank suddenly shook again and John helped him back to his bed.

"I think I should call someone." said John.

"No, no I've got what I need here. I'll take care of myself when you've left. You just remember what I said," said Frank.

"Well, I'll make you some tea at least."

There was small box of Lipton's Tea. John brewed Frank a cup. He spotted the tiny refrigerator by the bed and was gratified to find it clean on the inside and stocked with milk and margarine and a half a hamburger. John sat on one of the orange plastic chairs, and waited until Frank had drunk half of his tea. Frank's breathing had become more regular and his color returned.

The afternoon was shot. He went home and waited for Haidee to get home from work.

He didn't see Frank during the week. Jeff came in once, just at closing.

He didn't seem himself at all. Rather than planting himself at the counter and telling John about his latest schemes, he moved quickly and quietly, picking up a couple books from the legal section. They were books on wills. He wouldn't look John in the face.

"So you talked the old man into leaving you everything?" asked John. John couldn't imagine there was anything, except the stories. You can't leave anybody your stories.

Jeff looked up. "It's not your business. Someone needs to take care of him. It should be someone that understands what he has to offer. I can do a very good job being a caretaker. My lover died of AIDS four years ago. I am very patient. I am very understanding."

"You shouldn't take care of someone unless you love them. Not because they can give you something."

"Everyone eventually takes care of someone because of what someone gives them, even if it's love, or just a few good stories."

John said, "You better be sure that he has what you want."

"He's got this book called *Yoga for Bolsheviks*. This local Communist met a Mazatec shaman and learned the secret of dream control. You know the Mazatecs?"

John smiled, "Not personally, but they introduced the West to psilocybe mushrooms, morning glory seeds and salvia divinorum. Do I win the Oaxacan trivia contest?"

Jeff smiled. "You win. What no one knows is that they developed a practice similar to Tibetan dream yoga."

This should be a good deal for Frank, hell maybe he could cure Jeff of dreaming. Poe and ghost should work, but John couldn't stop himself. He poured himself a cup of coffee and asked Jeff, "Well here is your trivia, do you know Professor Joe Gould?"

"Is he an ethnologist?"

"He was a hobo panhandler, a Harvard graduate, a real character in the '40s."

Jeff made an attempt to look interested while putting a white and orange trade paperback of *The Complete Book of Wills, Estates and Trusts* by Alexander A. Bove Jr. Esq. on the worn wooden counter.

"The *New Yorker* ran a piece on him during World War II. 'Professor Seagull' He carried Big Chief tablets with him all the time—claimed to be writing *The Oral History of Our Time*—it was going to be a million word history of the people, the shirt sleeves multitude. He became enough of a legend that a *New Yorker* big shot followed him around. Turned out Professor Joe had both hypergraphia and writer's block. He just kept rewriting some trivial incidents of his life."

"Fascinating. What a deep parallel to my situation. I want to help an old man, and there have been other old men who are con artists. Why 'Seagull' anyway?"

"One of the ways Joe Gold earned money was making weird noises and dancing. He claimed to speak the language of the seagulls. He said he translated over ninety percent of Longfellow into sea gull. He said the poems sounded better in gull:

> "All the wild-fowl sang them to him,
> In the moorlands and the fen-lands,
> In the melancholy marshes.

Chetowaik, the plover, sang them—my great aunt won a prize at the Texas State Fair for declaiming the *Song of Hiawatha*. I imagine it would sound pretty great in gull. Look you like Frank, he has told me that you have given him dozens of paperbacks over the years."

"When the big shot wrote the article on Joe Gould, Joe became a caricature of himself. The big shot caught Joe's writer's block and then didn't write for thirty years."

Jeff said, "Just sell me the books. I've been a good customer. I won't need you any more."

John rang up the books.

"They're $18.85."

Jeff handed him a twenty and told him to keep the change.

Jeff did his best imitation of storming off.

When John told Haidee that night, she suggested that he was jealous,. Not many people adore Frank like you do. Maybe you want to be the only to do the good deeds for the old man. Maybe you think you are the only worthy of the stories.

After a week John decided to call on Frank. He went to the market and bought a selection of gourmet teas, five pounds of sugar and a fancy mug. He went up to Frank's apartment and knocked.

There was no answer.

He came back a few times in the afternoon. About five he was worried. He asked the young Korean man, who sold the cell phones shop if he had seen Frank. The man said that he had not seen Frank in a couple of days, but that was nothing unusual. Frank often spent three or four days alone in his room. John said he was going in, and the man said OK.

The door was unlocked.

Frank lay on the floor near the bed. It looked like he might have fallen. There was some blood, sticking his few white hairs to the greasy yellow linoleum. His eyes were open. The police spent two hours talking to John and the shopkeeper.

Jeff had left town.

He apparently left the night after he spoke to John.

It wasn't clear if violence was involved, and the police weren't very interested. A small article graced the *Austin American Statesman* focusing on Frank's involvement with the alternative press. John was surprised to find out that he had also ran a club in the seventies, which seemed to have been the high tide in his economic life. Club Zothique had burned to the ground in mysterious circumstances. Hints about organized crime were dropped in the article.

A week later the Korean man came to the New Atlantis shop.

"No one has come for his things. I asked the landlord and he said that you could have his things. I saw you cry when you found him, so I thought you were good enough."

John borrowed the key. He went with Haidee that night. Downtown is fairly quiet at night. They parked their van in front of the cell phone store. John unlocked the door and they went upstairs. The apartment hadn't been cleaned or organized in any way. No one had even washed away the small bloodstain, which seemed really sad. Haidee hugged him a moment and then they began putting books into a giant garbage bags. They would drop them off at the self-storage unit that John rented, on Sunday he would sort them out, and price the ones he thought he could sell. He'd give the rest to Goodwill.

Even though the little apartment had seemed full of books, certainly as crowded as the New Atlantis, it only filled two garbage sacks full. They were mainly old paperbacks—mysteries and SF. There was some hardback poetry and histories.

They were quiet during the sacking up of the books.

Haidee asked. "Would you like to be alone here for a while? I could go down the street to the Decline and have a cup."

"Yeah. I would."

She nodded and left.

He carried the two sacks full of books downstairs

and then went and sat on the bed. It wasn't a clear ending. Had Jeff killed him? Killed him for the book, or angry because there was no book? Had Jeff found him? Had Jeff just left his enthusiasm for Communist Yoga passed like all the others?

Had Frank had a good life?

He looked about the desk. He got up and opened it. Inside was a pile of mail. Junk mail and unpaid bills, and a big brown envelope with his name written on it in pencil. Inside was a small book, a cheaply made leather-bound book, and its title once golden had become verdigris-green. It was *Yoga for Bolsheviks* by James M. Cassutto.

Always leave 'em guessing.

John sat on the bed again, he would read for a few minutes and then join Haidee for a cup of tea and a slice of chess pie.

# WHAT ARE BEST FRIENDS FOR?

Steve wasn't surprised when Joan hit him up for a loan. Joan had been in and out of work for three years (and there was the custody thing), and rent was due in two days. So Steve lent her three hundred dollars against her computer. Steve drew up an elaborate paper of lien—he wasn't worried about the money, but he thought Joan might take her four-year-old son and split, and he wouldn't have a claim on the computer. It was a better machine than the piece of crap on his desk at home. But how good a computer did you need to visit porn sites and Robot Nine?

More importantly Joan was Sally's best friend, and Sally and he were beginning to look like a permanent alliance. Steve handed Joan three Benjamins and got her to sign the lien papers. Joan drove off to court to continue her eleventh hour custody battle, and Steve drove to work.

Texas Data Systems filled a three-story red-brick-and-gold-anodized-window building on a tree-shaded quiet street. Steve's "office" was a windowless cubicle near the center of the second floor. He began inputting changes on his manual, a novella-length description of a nine-pin to eighteen-pin interface. Juan, his chubby cube mate, sauntered in a few minutes after one.

Juan said, "Guess what?"

"What?" asked Steve.

"I sold the story I showed you to *Weird Tales*."

"Hey, congratulations."

Juan and Steve and a couple of other people, who had since moved on from TDS, had started writing or at least playing-at-writing two years ago, after taking a class at the New Atlantis bookstore. Well Juan had, Steve had only produced the beginnings of short stories, which remained in a manila folder in the bottom drawer of his desk. Steve stood up and shook John's sweaty pudgy hand. Steve didn't like fat people; they smelled. He had to be friends with Juan—he didn't want people to say that he was prejudiced. Steve and Juan made the rounds from cubicle to cubicle spreading the good news. People said all the things they say to people making their first sales. Be sure and tell us when it comes out. We'll all get a copy. We'll throw you a party. Someday there'll be a plaque on this building, "Juan Martinez worked here." Juan glowed all afternoon and Steve printed out his manual. Steve had his fun with this again that night, telling Sally at the Hunan Dragon.

"Juan was floating about two inches off the ground after he got the word."

"Whatever happened to your literary efforts?"

"Well. You know."

"Is that laziness or block?"

"Hey. You're supposed to be on my side, remember. I make more with technical writing than any fiction free-lancer I know. I may start up again anytime. Anyway I was able to loan Joan three hundred."

"Against her computer."

"Well it's not like it's worth it. She's the one who insisted. I was willing to lend it to her against her word. She's your best friend."

"You kept her from getting evicted. Currently she tells everybody that you are her best friend." Said Sally.

"Her best friend would be anyone that could give her a job. Maybe if she leaves town. The employment picture here sucks. And you know she's not leaving if she has to leave her kid entirely in the hands of her ex. She's licked."

"He's a real creep."

"Yeah. I've met him. Here comes our Chicken Kung Pao."

"That will all be over this Friday. The court decides custody then."

"I hope Joan copes if the court cuts Mickey out of her life. She was pretty wide-eyed at lunch."

Friday came. The court decided. Joan did not cope. Joan had purchased a cheap pistol at Snooper's Pawn for protection some months back. She discharged a bullet through the top of her soft palate.

Joan's father called Steve on Sunday afternoon. He'd found the lien and wanted Steve to come by and pick up the computer. Steve said that under the circumstances it would be O.K. for them to keep the computer. But they said they had no use for the thing—and it would help them clean up things if Steve got it. Besides Joan had told them what a good friend he was.

Steve was surprised how old Joan's parents looked. Death of an offspring must really suck away the years.

Joan's computer represented a step up from Steve's old machine. He had planned to upgrade for a while, but he was the sort that never spent a nickel unless necessary. Years ago when he did therapy, his shrink told him that he was cheap because he had no self-worth. He looked up a couple of college buds on Facebook, then before he went to bed he thought he should look for any really personal files and delete them. He wouldn't want someone reading his diary entries, or that bad love poetry he wrote for Sally, or finding the urls of his favorite porn sites.

He came upon two entries called "Games of Light and Dark" and "Allegro." He assumed that the first was a game package and the second to be a music-generating program. He called up "Games."

"Games of Light and Dark" proved to be a short story, a five-thousand-word tale of Egyptian adepts battling for the soul of a young psychic in modern-day Los Angeles. Car chases, gang wars, crack, incense, and the brief appearance of Set and Horus over the skies of east L.A. Good stuff really—except for the occasional dangling participle or lapse into passive. Editing habits die hard and Steve was changing this, and polishing that; before considering that this might not be his property. He hadn't even made a back up. The story was now in its new form; although, it could perhaps be reconstructed. He didn't know if he had just disrespected the dead. It was midnight, the traditional hour for such things.

His first impulse was to send it to Joan's parents. Then he realized that they won't understand it. Unlike many senior citizens the computer had not made it into their world, they had almost seemed sacred of it, fearing that it might send them down the information super highway. Then he thought of Mickey. He could sell the story and then put the money in a college savings account for Mickey. It all seemed so noble.

He would be everybody's hero. He got out the book he had bought on selling short fiction a couple of years ago. He put the story into MSS form and realized that he needed an address to send the story. Juan had a *Writer's Market*. He went to work half and hour early. He was going to do all this in secret, so that when it panned out he would look heroic. If it didn't pan out no one would ever know.

John's bottom drawer always sprang if you tugged hard enough. He wrote the *Fantasy & Science Fiction* address on the brown envelope, closed the drawer, and sprinted to the mail box in front of TDS. He shoved the envelope in just as Juan drove up on his beaten-up blue Toyota.

Juan said, "You're here early."

"I just wanted to mail the first fan letter for your *Weird Tales* story."

"You dummy. They haven't printed it yet."

"Oh they won't pay much attention to it anyway. I sent it out on your stationery."

Weeks passed and finally Steve got an acceptance from *F&SF*. His first story! It came with a two-page contract that talked about foreign rights and subsidiary book rights and lots of things Steve didn't understand. But he was able to find the dotted line. He told everybody. There was no **harm** in telling everybody, after all it would be appearing under his name. That had always been the plan. He should get some egorites here for everything. It wasn't like Joan had had the guts to send it out. Besides Mickey would get the money. He was sure that Joan's parents wouldn't approve, he could remember Joan telling him that they were some kind of fundies—surely not folks thrilled to see Egyptian gods on the cover of a magazine over their dead daughter's by-line. It was a good thing not to mention Joan.

When he got home he called up "Allegro." "Allegro" was a short novel—the quest of a young man looking for a rumored "lost" group of Bach manuscripts during the Cold War. The search took him on both sides of the Iron Curtain through gunfire, intrigue and two sets of hot romance with a vivid dream sequence in which he becomes Bach. With very little padding this could become a bestseller. Shiny and profitable in airport bookstores. And not without literary merit.

Steve began to pad.

He went to use bookstores and bought up tour

guides. He began to pour local color in. He re-adapted scenes from his favorite erotica; Joan had had a lace curtain approach to sexuality. Steve bought a copy of Douglas Hofstader's *Gödel, Escher, Bach: An Eternal Golden Braid* from the New Atlantis bookstore. Steve took liberal helpings from Hofstader's book on math and codes and patterns—it made a heady mix of sex and danger and pop science. He was excited by it.

He would break off from work, email a passage home (to Joan's old machine) People covered for him during the three weeks he expanded "Allegro" to novel-length. Especially Juan. Steve had never felt close to Juan, but Juan apparently really liked Steve. Juan's wife had died years before and apparently the little writer's workshop D. B. Bowen had run downtown had literally been the only place Juan had gone for pleasure in nearly ten years.

*Fantasy & Science Fiction* sent Steve a check for $206.00. Depositing half of it for Mickey—somewhere along the line he decided half was the appropriate share for his compensation—was a bother. It was such a small sum. He might have to explain things to his bankers. He'd wait until *Allegro* came out. Then he could make arrangements. After all he was a friend of Joan's. Everyone would understand why he wanted to help Mickey.

*Allegro* grew to 165,000 words; and by the first snowfall, Steve was sure that they were the perfect 165,000. He asked Juan for his *Writer's Market*. He was going to send the first three chapters and an outline to the twenty-five most likely publishers. Surely someone would show an interest. Juan opened his desk. Steve saw the pile of manuscripts underneath the bright yellow *Writer's Market.*

"What's that?"

"Oh. Just some stories I'm working on. I thought I'd get twenty or so together—you know, linked stories—then try to sell them to the magazines and then sell the whole lot as book."

"Are you finished with them?"

"I've got eighteen, I'm holding out for twenty-three. It's my lucky number."

"Yeah. I read *Illuminatus!* in college too."

"Hail Eris!"

"All hail Discordia!"

"Hey, best of luck with your book." said Juan as he slid his desk drawer shut.

*Aren't you people supposed to read* Bless Me, Última *or* George Washington Gómez?

During the weekend, Steve made much use of the office copy machine on the top floor of Texas Data Systems.. He made twenty-five piles of his first three chapters and outline. He had them on the floor, on desks, on chairs, atop filing cabinets. *I have made a fortress out of my words, if you want to play in my fort you have to be nice to me.* Maybe Steve's therapist had been right so many years ago, maybe the childhood abuse had lowered his emotional IQ. Or maybe he was a fucking genius. Stephen King's first name is Steve too. Fucking genius.

After wearing the clerk at Mockingbird Postal Station, Steve picked up Sally and headed to Garcia's. He slurped down food thick with green sauce. Sally fantasized about his novel, the film rights, the adventure game rights, etc. She could hardly wait to see what he would write next.

Neither could he.

Steve put his fragments on Joan's system. If he could finish one of them—put something together and finish one—it would be enough. It didn't have to be good. He considered looking for stories sufficiently old or obscure. He could rip-off their endings and fit to his beginnings. Plagiarism would be okay if it wasn't for lawyers. Dark-suited men with briefcases began to chase him in his dreams.

Juan, of course, was having no problem finishing his book. Stories nineteen, twenty, and twenty-one appeared on schedule. Everyone said they'd be such a famous pair, Juan Martínez and Steve Cruise. One of them would surely do the Hemmingway bit and write-up the early years. Everyone at TDS began to bask in the future light of that book of dead names. People began saving their best remarks for it. Their cubicle held an endless audition for immortality. Everyone made it sound so good, if only they could be writers. People asked them all the cliché questions. "Where do you get your ideas?" Steve stopped seeing Sally as often, told her he was writing. She was so supportive. She was such a bitch, if only she would complain then he would have a reason not to write. It was all he needed, all he wanted. They could have a big fight, and then he could swear off writing. She'd feel guilty, but making her feel bad was OK, because she made him feel bad always asking about his novel. She was the reason he couldn't write anyway. It was already her fault; she should pay with a little guilt.

A couple of publishing houses expressed an interest in *Allegro*. Steve shared the good news with John. Juan replied that he had finished the twenty-three stories and was about to send the book off. The magazine sales would only tie up the rights. Juan could have just been quiet; he could have just said nothing and let Steve have his moment, but no moments for Steve.

Steve said "We'll have a copying and mailing session on Saturday. We'll make this a little tradition. I'll mail out your book, you'll mail my next book and so on."

Juan said, "That's the nicest thing I've ever heard. I always felt we would be doing stuff like that. I'm not at all surprised about *Allegro*. I always knew you would be the writer.. Remember that day the Bowen gave us the little note cards?"

One of the first exercises. Bowen had handed out three by five inch pale blue index cards. He had written an emotion on each. Steve got ENVY. Then you had fifteen minutes to write a scene where the emotion was invoked by the character's actions. It was called Show Don't Tell. Steve's was the best; he knew then he was meant to be a writer.

Steve visited his blue haired, frail grandmother that evening, cheering the old lady up immensely. They watched TV and recollected that Steve used to drop by after school for a plate of warm cookies. This was a completely bogus recollection. Steve's grandma hated to cook. They were both caught up in TV grand-mothers. She fell asleep during a rerun of *The Golden Girls* and Steve took what he had come for—his late grandfather's heart medicine. Steve let himself out without any fuss.

At home Steve ground the medicine. He poured fifteen tiny white nitroglycerin tables into a makeshift mortar and (what-the-hell) added five pink digitalis pills. He crushed the tiny tablets into a fine powder—easy to do since heart medicines are finely crystal-lized to get into the bloodstream quickly. He added the mixture to a small amount of ground Folgers coffee. He shook, added a little salt, which would help cut the bitterness (he hoped).

Everything went smoothly on Saturday. Juan addressed all the envelopes, while Steve ran off a couple of copies of *Allegro*. Steve brewed coffee in the two employee coffee pots. Decaf for himself, poisoned for John. Juan always drank his coffee with spoons and spoons of sugar. Steve brought the cups in. They talked writing. Steve refilled John's cup.

Juan said, "This coffee is strong."

"I was a truck driver in college."

Steve kept talking about all the things that wannabe writers talk about. The potential for a series, TV, movies, foreign rights, gaming rights, book tours, hot babes that would not mind John's fleshy middle. Talk and pour and talk and pour,

"Let me Irish that up for you." Steve poured a little Baileys in the John's cup.

"Aren't you having any?" asked Juan.

"I'm the designated mailer. As soon as we are ready I will take these down to the post office. Ain't it cool?"

"My heart is beating like a kettle drum. I am so excited." Sweat hung in big drops on Juan's light brown forehead. He smelled funny—a sort of metallic smell. Steve assumed that it wasn't exactly the sweet smell of success.

"It's that eminent fame plus the caffeine, of course," said Steve, "You know you should really take care better care of yourself."

Juan looked guilty, "I've got a confession, dude. I am really diabetic. Type II. I don't tell anyone at work, because I really like scarfing down desserts at the monthly office birthday parties."

*Big fucking surprise:* El Gordo *is a diabetic.*

"No shit," said Steve, "I had wondered. I mean last month I must have seen you devour three slices of red velvet cake. Well maybe if you keep yourself healthy for your adoring fans."

"I haven't taken care of myself since my wife left me. I drink too much, eat too many fast sugars. When I started this writing thing, I thought that maybe life wouldn't be day after day at TDS and nights when I hoped I would just die in my sleep."

Steve said, "Writing brought the best out in me. No question. Say man you are looking a little like a slice of red velvet cake right now. Why don't you go on home? I can handle everything here."

"I am a little queasy. Is it hot in here?" Juan seemed disoriented

"It is really hot," lied Steve. "Come on let's get you home. Enough excitement today for my flan."

Juan made his ponderous way to the escalator.

"No. Come on take the stairs. You need to start taking care of yourself, baby steps you know."

"You are the only friend I've got."

"I know. Joan used to feel the same way."

Steve began leading the bug man to the stairwell. With the slightest shiver of distaste, he put his hand on the sweat soaked back of Juan's pink shirt. Big, wet brown. As Juan began to step on to the straits, Steve sharply increased the pressure of his arm on John's back. Suddenly Juan ripped. He tried to break his fall, but only broke his arm. The body slumped-and-slid down to the turn in the stairs. Steve slowly stepped down to his fallen companion. Juan's heart had not withstood the strain. Poor Juan, he should have started that aerobics program he was always talking about. All those enchiladas and *tres leche* cake hadn't helped either. Lesson to us all. Steve gathered up Juan's envelopes and the MSS. He washed his coffee cup and put it on the rack—careful to leave the coffeepot turned on. Almost nothing was left in the bottom of the pot. He threw away the now almost empty Folgers's can that had the poison in it.

He was Juan's loudest mourner. Everyone had

known how close they were. Someone asked about Juan's book. Steve said that he thought Juan had sent it out. Juan had always been secretive about his writing. No, Steve had never seen the book. The family up from San Antonio had never heard of it. The boss saw how upset Steve was, and sent him home for a week to get over his loss. Steve used this time to print out new copies of John's work and stuff them into the envelopes that Juan had so thoughtfully provided. He changed the byline and the title and cleaned up Juan's grammar. Juan had chosen a good set of markets, but then Juan had an excellent understanding of his own work. Steve felt that *Borges at the Mike* could be a bestseller. It was funny and gritty and had a little magical realism as a seasoning. Nice salsa for a white boy. American *sabor*.

Bluebonnets azured the highways, and Steve's agent Mary Denning finalized a deal with Bantam for *Allegro*. *Borges at the Mike* was receiving a few enquires as well. Steve spent some of his generous advance on a three-strand pearl necklace for Sally. He showed it around the office and everyone said that he should quit and work full time. Nobody talked about Juan anymore. The consensus was that he'd never had a book in the first place. The strain probably killed him. Even Steve let himself be convinced.

Steve took Sally to Joaquin's, the only restaurant in town with a three star rating. She was so proud. She was going to try her hand at this. She already had an idea for a fantasy novel.

As he put the pearls around her neck, Steve wondered

how good it would be.

# RING OF THE RED KNIGHT

I hadn't liked the old man. Winslow Carvenell was a nuisance. Always measuring the border between our garden plots with a ruler—as though fearful a single tomato of mine might have cast a shadow over his roses. He was the most disagreeable sort of neighbor, and except for our mutual interest in the magical arts there was little in common between us. Neither of us were great enchanters, neither had great wealth. I had made my own through hard work and study, but an accident of birth had made my neighbor poorer than his kin.

But I was grieved when I heard he died and fearful when I heard it was murder. After all, he lived next door.

Shina, his maid, had found him with a cut from ear to ear. Someone had murdered him in his sleep. The maid, being resourceful, had called upon the constable before alarming the neighborhood. I heard of old Winslow's death from him, but I knew I would hear all the gory details from her—for Shina had once been a love of mine.

Constable Gager arrived just as I was heading off for the Academy where I taught classes in thaumaturgy,

beginning philosophy of magic, and magical episte-
mology. The constable had been a student of mine,
years ago. I had failed him because he was too lazy
to apply himself. He had improved with the passing of
years, but his hatred for me had certainly not dimin-
ished. Such is often a teacher's fate. He was suspicious
of the fact that I had heard nothing, and advised me
grimly not to leave town.

I was late for class, and some of my students had
walked. So I conjured a small pink cloud in my like-
ness and sent it off to the tavern where they were sure
to have gathered. It rounded them up in a few minutes,
and I gave a fairly good lecture on beginning invis-
ibility.

Shina was waiting for me when I got home. I had
given her the word which unlocked my door when we
were an "item" years before.

"It was awful, Robert," she said. "He was slumped
over his writing desk his throat slit from ear to ear.
His journal is ruined, who knows how many years of
research on his family is gone."

"Who do you think killed him?"

"Winslow didn't have an enemy in the world. Oh
you and he argued over trifles, and Dieter Betz over
at Miracle University argued over how to decipher
certain ancient texts, and he's never been too sweet
on his nephew, which is sad since the Count will be
paying for his funeral."

"William pays for everything after all. Did Winslow
have anything to bequeath?"

"His books and scrolls will go to the University. William came by and said he'd pay my salary for another month and that I could have any personal effects I wanted."

"I'm really sorry, Shina, if there's anything I can do—" That is probably the oldest incantation in mankind's repertory—its magic had been used up centuries before Atlantis sank beneath the waves. But she put her head on my shoulder and cried softly for a very long time. I saw quite a few silver hairs in her blond hair and wondered how I had become an old scholar. Where was the young wizard I once was? How long had I played the part of aging scholar-mage?

\* \* \* \* \* \* \*

The next day Count William paid me a visit. William was Winslow's nephew. William was the son of Rudolfo, the older of twin brothers. Rudolfo got the title and lands by arriving four minutes before his brother. Winslow got a scholar's salary and a small house from the university—one of the Count's favorite charities. William was a good Count, I suppose, he gave great feasts and his costume parties in Carnival season were well known. He dropped by my humble home to borrow texts, commission poetry or merely to give brandies and wines. But I never stood in his presence without knowing to my very bones that I was in front of the man who owned me. It is said the mark of a good ruler is that their presence makes you want to serve, but that a poor ruler merely makes you know that you serve.

Count William asked if I would deliver Winslow's eulogy. I accepted. He also told me that Constable Gager had a lead on the case. Someone had seen the murderer leaving Winslow's home.

It would be a grand funeral, promised Count William, he would spare no expense.

I began to work on Winslow's eulogy. As is always the case when someone dies, I wished that I had paid more attention to him in the living years. His scholarship had been great. I really wished that he had finished his history of his own family.

I was pondering this loss to learning when Shina came running into my yard. I let her in.

"Robert. It wasn't you, was it? Tell me you didn't kill him."

"Of course I didn't kill him. Why would you think something that crazy?"

She reached out her right hand to me, opening it from the fist it had been. In her palm was the ring of the red knight.

"Have you told anyone?" I asked.

"No. Not yet. If you didn't do it, someone wants it to look like you did. I found it under the table; I was cleaning up the house. I didn't know if I should take it to you or to Gager."

I reached for the ring, but she made the fist again.

"You've got to give it to me—so I can figure out what's going on."

"What if you did drop it?"

"Shina, you know me."

"I know. I don't know. What are the rules for murder and friendship? I don't know. I should take it to Gager."

"If you do, you'll be putting a noose around my neck. Leave it with me for a night, I may be able to get the ring to talk."

"You're not that powerful a wizard, Robert, you know that."

"Sometimes a person can be pretty powerful if his life is in danger."

She started to release the ring.

"You must promise me," she said, "that you'll give me the ring tomorrow. I can say I just found it. I don't want to be jailed for having interfered with a criminal case."

"I promise."

She handed me the ring, a simple circle of red gold with the word "judge" written in the High Speech. She made me promise several more times. She was scared, but I was terrified.

The red knight, Sir Starkad, had been a harsh man. My father, the swineherd, used to say that the best words that could be spoken of a man were "He was tough, but fair." Starkad would not have needed "fair"—his justice was harsh.

* * * * * * *

Let me tell you about the ring. Last year at Carnival, Count William invited all of us poor teachers to a great costume ball and feast. Now, as you know, a scholar will not pass up a free meal for any reason. I dressed up as Sir Starkad, the founder of the Count's family. I had a replica of the ring made as a magical focus so that I could conjure up the rest of the costume. I had even won a small prize for best costume (historical).

Winslow, the only person to attend the party without costume, had nothing but bad things to say about my choice. Who was I, a commoner, to wear (even in sport) the arms of a noble family? Count William announced a special prize for his uncle: Best Curmudgeon.

A few months after Carnival, I was looking for the ring. I wanted to melt it down for the gold so I could buy a particularly wonderful set of scrolls from Mordrake. I couldn't find the ring, and chalked up the loss to my messy bachelor life. I hadn't thought to tell anyone of my loss. Not that it would matter. The ring at the site of Winslow's murder could convince any jury. He had complained widely of my presumption in wearing it.

In one of my books of magic was a spell to open the mouth of objects. It would cause a thing to reveal its history. A very advanced spell, this—but if I could discover the killer, I might be able to slip the noose. I hated the killer whoever she or he was. He (or she) had stolen my best enemy and wanted to frame me.

The spell was a simple one. It involved a red oil lamp with a wick upon which had been written certain characters and a few barbarous names. I performed it an hour after sunset. Nothing happened. I put a new wick in the lamp and tried again, pouring all of my magical strength into the operation. Nothing happened.

I felt weak and sad. I blew out the lamp, leaving the ring on my writing desk. I walked heavily over to my cot and threw myself down to sleep. I dozed off quickly. Then I heard or thought I heard the chair at my writing desk being pushed back. I couldn't see in the darkness of my house, but I felt like someone was sitting at my table. I thought I heard someone writing.

"Shina?"

Nothing.

"Winslow?"

Still nothing.

I sprang up and ran over to the desk. No one seemed to be there. I lit a candle. No one there. But didn't I leave the ring near the *center* of the table?

I decided I was having a really bad case of nerves. I left the candle lit and returned to bed. Amazingly I fell asleep again, as if something in the room drove away consciousness.

I dreamed a little dream. I dreamt first of rings. Rich noble rings sparkling with gems of this and other worlds. Poor couples' wedding bands. Slaves rings from the southern deserts. Each of them rolling endlessly through the night. Each of them a symbol of something the wearer was bound to. Each rolling like the cycles of our lives from birth to death to be given to another in another life. Rolling along, controlling the paths of the life of the person wearing them. I was somewhere far above them watching them as bodiless observer, but I began to sink toward them, and the sound of their rolling grew into a great roar. I feared I would land among them and be worn to bits by their endless rolling. By this time I was thinking that the rings *and all they implied* ruled mankind. Who was the first to pledge his troth over a band of metal? Once that pledge was made, we lived in a world of meanings, a world where things could be done with words like "I do" or "I swear." I was falling into the great river of rings which had rolled since my ancestors' ancestors had decided to live by Law. How could I withstand that force? I had avoided the force by becoming a scholar, a semi-recluse, but now that world of men—with its endless rings—would have me.

I fell but as is the way of dreams, merely woke. I was awake for an instant thinking that I saw something sparkle upon my desk and then I returned to sleep.

I must have slept a great while for I know that my second dream was near dawn.

I dreamt I was at a masked ball in Count William's home. I was dressed as the red knight, but there was another red knight. I approached this man angry at having my costume aped. The other red knight lurked in the shadows. When I came upon him I saw that his armor was not the festive stuff of Carnival fantasy. Battle had left its mark.

He raised his visor and I saw in inexpressible sadness in his gray eyes. I wanted to say something to offer some assurance to this man who suddenly seemed like a brother to me. I thought he has chosen the world of rings, not a do-nothing scholar like me. He lowered his visor and made his way through the crowd toward the throne. Some grave matter of state was unfolding.

I thought to follow him, but the masked crowd seemed suddenly thicker and noisier. I doubted that I could pass through them.

I looked for a pathway close to the walls. It was then I saw old Winslow sitting at his writing desk penning a manuscript. I'll tell him that I'm sorry he's dead, I thought, for such thoughts are in the way of dreams.

I made my way to him.

He was writing in his usual beautiful hand:

A History of the Carvenells

*The first of the line prepares the last of the line's doom.*

\* \* \* \* \* \* \*

I woke suddenly because something cold touched my cheek. *Rolled* over my cheek. The candle had gone out. I sprang out of bed looking for what had touched me. I threw my bedding aside on the floor feeling for something small. I found nothing. Then I went and got a candle, my fingers shaking as I put flint to steel. By its light I saw nothing, but the ring was gone from the desk.

I began lighting candles. I would flood my small house with light. I must find the ring before tomorrow. I had no doubt that Shina, already unsure in her resolve to let me have the ring, would tell Constable Gager of her find.

I went through every nook and cranny. I unrolled my scrolls, threw down my books, forced my fingers into every chink in the walls. I looked under my washbasin, in my glasses, among my silverware. It was nowhere. The ring had rolled away, and with it no doubt any chance of my avoiding the noose.

I resolved right away to pack and leave the country. I could perhaps manage a spell to fly away—of course I would have to leave most of my treasures here. My precious books and scrolls! The wealth of a lifetime of learning.

I was packing a satchel when the knocking began. I had never heard so loud a series of knocks in my life.

"Open up, Robert Griffith. I have come to arrest you for the murder of Winslow Carvenell. If you don't open this door, I shall break it down."

I uttered the word, which opened the door.

"Caught you before you could leave!" boomed Constable Gager.

With him were Count William, a tear-stained Shina, and a burly peasant man I'd seen once in the farmer's market.

"This man says he saw a figure dressed in red armor leaving the home of Winslow Carvenell and going toward your door. When I questioned Shina Auw she broke down and confessed having found the ring from your costume at the scene of the murder, and giving you said ring during a period of poor judgment."

I had to hand it to Gager, a lesser man couldn't have boomed his way through an utterance so long. At least if I am hung swiftly, I thought, I would not have to listen to his annoying voice too long.

"Where is the ring that Shina Auw gave you?" asked Gager.

I was pondering the reply when Count William walking past the constable said, "Here. On his desk."

There was the ring all right. Had it been there all along mocking the mind I was clearly losing?

The Count walked to my desk. He reached to grab it, when it seemed the ring of its own accord rolled over and slipped onto his hand.

"No," he said, "It's a trick. It isn't my ring. It's his. I didn't steal it from him. I didn't."

The Count's face was white with fear. He was trying to pull off the ring but couldn't manage it. Blood poured from his finger.

The Constable hesitated, not know whether to grab the Count or me or both.

The Count's struggle was both comic and terrifying. He bellowed in pain and rolled on the floor as thought fighting a score of men. A huge bear of a man—his fight against a simple band of gold made no sense. I have heard few men be really afraid. Men talk about fear, or whisper about their fears, but only animals whimpered like this. I was appalled and enthralled.

The Count said, "I'll confess. I killed him.. Just get the ring off. It bites."

The Constable ordered me to remove my spell from the ring. I started to say that I hadn't put any spell on it, but then I remembered my failed invocation from the night before. I said a couple of words to end the enchantment.

The ring came off, and the Constable took the Count away. The ring had bitten the Count severely; his finger was hanging on only by a scrap of bloody skin. I guess the enchantment had opened its mouth.

Over the next few months we learned the story. Winslow Carvenell had discovered a document describing the birth of the twins. The first-born twin had a large birthmark on his back, the younger was unblemished. Winslow, with the ugly strawberry-colored blotch on his left shoulder, was the true heir. The doctor who had delivered the children had mixed up the details later, and the old count was happier with an unblemished heir anyway.

Winslow had approached William asking for the title and lands. After all, Winslow would only get to enjoy it for a few years, and then it would pass back to William. William didn't want to relinquish power—even for a few months to the grumpy old scholar. He decided to slay his uncle.

He knew that I had often quarreled with old Winslow. One day the Count had visited me hoping to find some way to incriminate me. I remember he had asked to borrow some ancient book of poetry, as I had searched among my badly organized library he noted that I was using the ring as a paperweight. This proved to him that I didn't know the value of gold, and was therefore unworthy of it. Or at least was unaware if it. He stole the ring to plant in the scene of his crime.

William resides in the king's dungeons, where I hear he has very bad dreams. The fonder of the line, the red knight, had been known for fearsome forms of justice. Apparently William dreams himself as a guest in his ancestor's dungeon-courts.

I live much as I did before, but increasingly wonder if I should die ring-less. Now that I have penned this little story, perhaps I should try a sonnet for Shina.

Shall I compare thee to the mystery of dream?

Thou are more mysterious and more rare.

A good start....

# THE SYRINGE

Mr. Randolph Holland's prize possession was an old-style glass hypodermic syringe. It had served him and his habit well for twenty-five years. Despite what you may have read on the subject, junkies can live a very long time—long, anonymous, gray lives in cheap boarding houses—with two-bit jobs which have only the function of serving the monkey. Such syringes used to be the rule, but plastic with its disposability now dominated the market.

"Never misses the vein," he used to boast. "Always hits blood."

Mr. Randolph Holland not only lost his prize possession but also his life (although in a sense he had lost it years before) to a pair of the street thugs named Crazy Eddy and Rico.

"Man, this guy didn't have shit," said Eddy cleaning out the boarding room with leisure. Mr. Holland had been quiet about his going, so the boys weren't worried that his neighbors would be dropping in. They had watched the old junkie.

"Let's pull him off the bed," said Rico. "We can stay here for a while, sell his shit tonight."

They pulled him off the bed. Rico took out a package of condoms and they amused themselves.

Later as night fell, Rico asked, "You want to shoot up his stash? There ain't enough to sell."

"Nah, I don't do that stuff. Makes you too slow."

Rico was more catholic in his tastes than Eddy. As he prepared his fix, he said, "I ain't never seen a syringe like this. I bet that old cocksucker used this for years man. Look the metal's *green* on the handle. I wouldn t stick it in me."

"I washed it man. What are you worried about. Maybe it's haunted. Maybe it's used to biting the blood of the living every night." Rico managed a pretty good Lugosi for the word *blood*. He filled the syringe from the spoon, and tied off his right forearm.

"Don't talk that stuff with him stuffed under the bed."

"We didn't wake him up before, we're not going to wake him up now."

Rico went to shoot up. Suddenly his arm jerked and the syringe plunged full into his shoulder.

"Shit."

He injected the entire contents and then pulled at the hypo. The plunger on the back came out and blood pouredf rom the device.

"Shit! Shit! Shit!"

He was loud, very LOUD.

All Eddy could think of to do was hit hard. Ring his bells. Quiet him down. He punched Rico's nose, and Rico fell.

Eddy didn't even breathe for a while. Just listened. There were people talking, and toilets flushing, and TVs—but no knock on the door.

He checked Rico. Rico was not going to get up.

He would stay here a few hours, then clear. He gathered up the money from the two bodies, and he turned off the lights so it would look like no one was home.

It was a long wait. Everytime he heard somebody in the hall, he damn near pissed himself. All he could think of was "drinks the blood of the living." What a stupid bastard to say something like that. Better not think it too much.

He wondered how many times the needle had tasted blood. Once a night for—he couldn't figure it out. When would the blood become a habit for the needle, like junk for the junky?

Something rolled in the floor. Someone had kicked the needle. Oh god, should he risk the light. Stupid son of a bitch. Stupid—

That was his last clear thought as he felt the needle prick his arm.

# MY HEART
# SHIFTING AS SAND

My capture had been the irony of ironies.

War was newly upon us, and I had seen its strange fever grow in Naema. It had grown in many of our friends, but we had young children, which should be a cure for the fever. At first I had argued with her. I did not feel the need to rid "our country" of the French. "Our country" was drawn on a map in Europe. The French were newcomers, much as we Arabs were newcomers taking land from the Berbers. If we drove the French away, surely the Berbers would drive us away?

My arguments fell on deaf ears, or rather ears full of new words, that packed them as tightly as the wax packed in the ears of Odysseus's sailors. I found a sublime solution. I would take her to see her family in the South, in the Haut Plateau. It is not like the North. Nothing thrives in the southern *wilayat*, and she would see that life is more precious than principle. Her family lived here in a miserable little village, she would see her mother fussing over the children, and she would yearn not to put them in danger. This was good, because the war will not last. France will win.

I shed my Western clothes for the trip. We would go as Arabs to see Arabs. There was a small bus that runs into the Plateau once a week, and Naema, the children and I boarded it. She did not chatter about the war as we drove into the sea of sand. She spoke of her mother, of favorite foods and games. She taught songs to the children. As the sight of sand became everything, lines drawn on a map could not bother her. The bus climbed onto the snow-covered Plateau and her spirit soared like a desert falcon. I had always found the emptiness oppressive, perhaps it mirrored emptiness within me. So as she told our children the stories of Ali and Fatima, I entered into a silent dream of her family reunion. I could see her mother running to meet us, her stupid brother with his rotten smile, the cousins and hangers-on joyous because a fatted goat would be slain. I heard the laughter and tasted the hot sweet tea, and the showing of family treasures.

The land of the Plateau lies flat and stretches as far as is painful. The snow, as a white as blank page made it worse. I knew that history, that old enemy of mankind, hungered to write something here. We saw the village long before we arrived. There was no one to meet us, but from the bus we could see her mother sitting in her doorway, her veil tossed overhead, crying loudly. I held the children back, while Naema ran to her mother. Behind us the bus drove on, stranding us here for a week.

Her brother, in his stupidity, had killed a cousin because of a minor quarrel, and was now hidden in the desert. Her mother was alone, the more distant family members having suddenly found reasons to be else-where.

She looked dully at the chocolate we had brought, the tea and the olive oil. We moved in, and we began telling her that she would have to come to the city with us. Life is too hard in the South for an old woman. She had the arguments that you expect—her friends were here, she must wait for her son; she could not survive in the noise of the city. But she knew and we knew that she would be joining us in a week.

We went to bed. It seemed that I had no more than closed my eyes, when the house was filled with sound. A gendarme came looking for the fugitive brother. He knew a man was in the house, he had seen, he was nobody's fool. Naema was yelling he was mistaken that I was her husband fresh arrived from the city, and I was staring a gun pointed at my face, being told to rise and dress.

The gendarme said that I did not dress as a city dweller.

And that was that.

Since my lot was cast before I could speak, I chose not to speak. I knew his type, the same sort of bureau-crat that I deal with everyday. There would be no argu-ment. I would be held until Saturday and then sent by bus to the city where all things would be resolved. So I went along meekly. I would sleep in the jail. Not much different than my mother in law's, except that I could perhaps hope for a more comfortable bed. Besides this served my plan well. Naema would see the sort of things the war could lead to and abandon her notions.

However the gendarme awakened me at dawn. I kept up the pretence I could not speak French, and he told me in halting Arabic that I must go with him to school. In did not understand this sudden need for education, but saw his gun as checkmate in our little game.

He tied my hands together and we set off. He rode on a donkey and I was pulled behind, at a very slow pace, so that I could walk unhurt. Suddenly I realized that we were leaving the village. Perhaps he meant to kill me, I would be sad to die where I could not see a tree or any green thing. I was very tired I tried to tell myself that I would be dying for the sake of my family, because I thought if I had a reason, I would at least have inner way out of this absurd situation.

I walked a long way. Longer than I had ever walked. Maybe I would simply walk across the great emptiness and dissolved into it. The gendarme began to speak to me. Since he thought I was ignorant of his tongue I known that he merely talked to fill the void with words.

He was Corsican, a countryman of Napoleon. He tried to tell me what good things the French had brought to the land. How their law was better than Berber law or Islamic law. How I would have a trial and every-thing would be fair.

I liked it better then there was only silence in the vastness. The snow was thin, but it made my feet very cold.

At last we came to another village, so like the one

had left I wondered if we had merely gone in circles.

We went to a schoolhouse where a pale and weak looking schoolmaster signed for me like a shipment of grammar books. I listened to them discuss me. Was I one of the rebels? The schoolmaster was to deliver me to yet another village, where perhaps justice waited for me. Like a camel they tied me to a post outside of the school. The schoolmaster showed me his sidearm, no doubt useful in classroom discipline.

After a decent interval the gendarme departed and the schoolmaster took me inside the tiny school. I could see that he didn't want to have me. He did not relish the job of jailor. I realized that many French might be as uncommitted as I. Perhaps together we could muster enough apathy to leash the dogs of war.

He fed me, and told me in passingly good Arabic that he too was born here. The words did not inspire any brotherly feelings in me. He asked why I had done it. By "it' he meant of course the stupid murder by my stupid brother-in-law. So I muttered some nonsense. He did not ask me my name. I doubt that Arabs often have names, but then I did not ask his.

He took me to his bedroom for the night, pointing at a cot with his pistol, which by now I was sure had never been and would never be fired. I undressed and lay down. He did the same and shortly thereafter began to snore. Sleep did not come to me. I am not an adventurous man. I did not know how to plan an escape, or consider that I could pull the pistol from his sleeping hand, and make my get away. Where would I go? If

I fled I would be a criminal. If I went through this charade I could possibly clear my name. I lay awake until I needed to make water.

I rose and went to the courtyard.

There in the moonlight was Naema, her brother and another man.

She spoke quietly and quickly, "Don't worry Fadlan! Tomorrow he will take you to Tinguit. We will be on the road and free you. Courage. We can't take you now."

They turned and ran into the moonlight. So strange had the scene been to me, that I stood there wondering if it had been a dream. It was not a scene from my life, and all I wanted was the scenes from my life back. I made my water and returned to my bed.

We rose the next day. I saw that he was lost as I was. We were brothers in our lack of commitment. I wanted to say something, but what can you say to your reluctant captor? My numbness, my emptiness comes out when I opened my mouth. I let him tie me up and he lead me out of the village to a limestone cliff at the edge of the Plateau. He had taken me to a path, one branch leading east and the other south. He surveyed the two directions. There was nothing but sky on the horizon. Not a man could be seen. He turned toward me, and I tired to share my emptiness with him. He could at least know that he was leading one like himself. He handed me a package. Not understanding I took it. "There are dates, bread, sugar. You can hold out for two days. Here are a thousand francs too," he said, "Now look there's' the way to Tinguit. You have a two-hour walk. At Tinguit you'll find the administration and the police. They are expecting you." He took my elbow and turned me rather roughly towards the south. "That's the trail across the Plateau. In a day's walk from here you will find the pasturelands and the first nomads. They'll take you and shelter according to their law."

I thought I should tell him that I would be saved by my family if I went east. I wanted him to know that it was not too late to avoid action, which will only take us form the things we love. That we could hold onto our routines and not have war. Because when war comes, it will eventually call us to its service. "Listen," I began.

"No, be quiet," He said. And he was still the man with the gun, even if he did not believe in that which had given the gun to him. He waked away. I headed east. I saw him look at me with some something like horror.

I laughed, but I knew he could not hear, in fact could not hear when he had been standing besides me. I was walking to a temporary peace, but war would swallow us up. The day would come when I would believe and he would believe, and an unseen hand will lift all the chess pieces on the board, and our silent days of waiting and our nights of dreaming our own strange games would end.

# THE JOY OF COLA

It was Austin, Texas, but it could have been any-where in the shadow worlds.

The crazy kids were the same age as Bill. They lived across the street in the dirtiest worst smelling house he had ever seen., It had a graywater system that meant they used their bathwater to poop in, and they only flushed when there was a lot of poop and the whole damn house smelled like ma privy. The kids were activists. The leader of the pack was some girl that got books for prisoners. Project Inside Out or Upside Down or some damn thing. Not educational books, books by Stephen King and murder mysteries. Yeah those guys need that. They were in prison, they aren't supposed to read.

Bill never had any damn time to read. He worked for $10.00 an hour which meant he could pay his mort-gage, buy his diabetes medicine and have basic cable. He used to read. The girl had come by yesterday asking him for used paperbacks. He had offered her *The Book of Mormon*. He wasn't Mormon, but the kids further down the street kept dropping them off. The girl was offended and went off about loving prisoners. He shut the door in her face.

He plopped down in his cheap (bur clean!) recliner and watched TV. It was from another planet where you could achieve bliss by drinking Pepsi. There was this girl with a pierced navel dancing. It was the girl from across the street. He had seen that navel. She must be rich. Some trendy star that was slumming in the gray water swamp. The Joy of Pepsi. He thought about jacking off to the image, but was too tired and just went to sleep.The next morning he had a plan. He would kidnap the girl, and hold her hostage to Pepsi. He wouldn't be hard ass about it. He didn't want her to suffer. For the first time in three years he called in sick, and then he went to New Atlantis Used Books and bought all of the Stephen King and Rex Hull books. He read the sections on kidnapping in the Hull books and  bought the duct tape. He put the soap in the sock and then he put a letter in their mailbox asking that Brittany drop by he had books for her. Then he went out and bought a case of Pepsi and one of Pepsi Light.

It was four in the afternoon when she came by. Her long red hair was done up in the filthiest dreds he had ever seen. A little pus oozed out around her navel ring.

"Come in." he said, "The books are in the back."

She followed him back to his bedroom, which no woman had done in two years. He pulled the sock form one pocket and the soap from another pocket and put the soap in the sock. She crossed the threshold and he swung.

She didn't have the decency to fall down, just yelled.

The filth and ropes of her hair probably softened the blow. He had to swing twice (and twice as hard ) to knock her out,. She had been beginning to turn, so the last blow hit just above her left eye and broke the skin. She was a vegan, so she didn't weigh much. He picked her up and put her in the old straight back chair that had belonged to his grandmother. He thought of it as the only nice thing that he owned, not understanding it had been poor people's furniture when she had bought it during the great depression.

He taped a funnel to her mouth so he would be to pour in the Pepsi. Then he tied a rope around her to be extra sure she couldn't escape, when she came to.

He figured it would be a bad idea to call from home. So he went to the 7-11. Not the close 7-11, he wasn't that dumb. He carried a can of Pepsi with him to call the 1-800 number for questions or concerns.

The phone tree presented him with many options: * For an extension; 1 For information about products, 2 For an explanation of how coke is different than Pepsi; 4 How to buy Pepsi products; 5 How to tell if you were a member of the Pepsi generation; 6 How to register complaints against Pepsi truck drivers; 7 How to register complaints about dead mice in bottles; 8 How to register complaints about other foreign objects in bottles; 9 How to present claim about kidnapping Brittany Spears. He pushed 9.

"Sorry, but our records show that Ms. Spears has not been kidnapped today, so we can not process kidnapping claims."

The recorded voice crushed Bill. He could not believe it. Perhaps he had been too hasty, perhaps there were other young women with pierced navels. He had missed a day of work in tight economy, which wasn't good, and he should probably have to let the girl go. Keeping for a sex-slave would mean cleaning and feeding her. He hadn't even let her go to the bathroom. Probably if he let her use his clean good-smelling bathroom she would be so happy that she would forget the little kidnapping incident.

He felt really tired and victimized by the time he got home. He wanted to nap, but decided to let the girl go.

She looked mad, so he through he would talk to her and then let her go to the bathroom, and then everything would be OK.

"Look," he said. "I know you probably aren't very happy right now. But I'll give you the books and I'm going to let you poop in my bathroom, and everything will be swell. I had a little senior moment and I thought you were Brittany Spears."

When he said Brittany Spears, her eyes softened and see looked sad.

He pulled the duct tape from her mouth.

"I am Brittany Spears." She said.

"No. The phone message says you're not."

"That's because I have been out of circulation long enough, shit-head." She said affectionately. "Just keep me for a few more hours and you can get a quarter mil."

"It's not really money that I want." Said Bill.

"I know, baby." She said, "Can you say what you really want?"

"I. I. I. Well money would make it better." Bill finally said.

"That's because money partakes of the Real." Said Brittany.

"What I really want is someone to love me enough to give me used Stephen King books."

"I Love you. I so Love this world that I send images of the Real World I come from into it."

"I don't understand." Said Bill.

"Here put your head on shoulder and I will tell about the Real World."

Bill put his head on her shoulder, which wasn't easy since he kneel down by the chair she was tied in. And so Brittany told Bill of the Real World. In the Real World people danced when they drank a good beverage. Everyone was healthy and good looking. Cars drove through endless fields on bright starry nights. Little lizards helped you get car insurance, and little dogs helped you have great intercultural dining experiences, and everyplace was really and truly Disneyland.

"People from your world discovered the Real World when they invented television. There are no TV channels,. No broadcasting. We came up with those myths, so you wouldn't feel bad watching the Real World. The Real World is commercials."

"But why would you ever leave?"

"Your world is very interesting to us. It's like a roller-coaster. Besides you people treat us well."

"But you're living in a dump."

"It's just a game for me. You've heard of other people from my world that live among you. For example the cast of *Different Strokes*."

"Is there anyway I can go to your world?"

"Of course Bill, we discover people all the time. Take the rope and off so that I can get out of this chair."

"Oh right. Sorry."

Brittany stood up and rubbed her wrists. Then she stretched her knees and arced her legs.

"What you have to do Bill is drink all of that Pepsi while I dance."

As soon as she started dancing she looked better. Her thick dreds become long flowing hair. Her dirty kin became clean. The pus vanished from her navel ring. By the time Bill was on his third Pepsi he could hear the music. His house seemed larger. His furniture became bigger, newer, more conformable, more fashionable. The air smelled better. He drank and drank and drank; although it became harder with each can. There were other people dancing with Brittany now. The roof of his house vanished and above was the bluest sky he had ever seen, with more perfect white sun above. The birds sang in time with swelling music. Flowers began to grow out of his floor. He drank and drank and drank. It really hurt. The President was walking up and beside him the Pope was roller-skating. People of all colors were dancing together. Good looking people. People better looking than anybody he had ever seen. He drank and drank. Soon the case would be finished.

Boy did it hurt. He really needed to go to the bath-room. He hoped they had bathrooms in the Real World. There was a talking lizard. There was the talking dog. It was all too wonderful. He could see the Pillsbury Doughboy in the distance dancing, dancing, dancing. One more can. He popped the top. He took a slug.

Bill's gut exploded. He had a moment to look down at the ragged hole that blood and Pepsi were gushing out of. Then he died and slowly began to fade from the Real World.

Brittany and her friends were laughing, but with his last breath he thought that he could detect some compassion in her voice. Maybe not enough to buy him a used copy of *The Shining*, but at least *Carrie* or one of the short story collections.

# OUR NOVEL

Upon my recent diagnosis with Carson's Syndrome, I realized that it was time to talk about the creation of *Wilson Is Not Toast*, which has the dubious distinction of being mentioned in every book on the oddball novels of the early twenty first century. *Wilson is Not Toast* did very well, even being a Mystery Club Book of the Month and having translations into twenty languages and adaptations for the WWW, film, TV and other media. If you are at all a mystery reader, you probably have a copy at home. What makes *WINT* so interesting is that it had eleven co-authors. Jointly written books seldom do well, but the author list for *WINT* has several other peculiarities. Firstly all of the authors had had only publishing credit before the publication of *WINT*, in a regionally distributed short story collection, which was aptly described as "dreadful vanity publishing at its worst." Secondly despite the huge success of the book only three of the writers went on to publish anything thereafter and their minor attempts were frankly published because of their connection with the successful *Wilson Is Not Toast*. I was the best published of the three.

I am Moses Gubb, and I on from my success with *WINT* into a writing "career" of seven mystery short stories and cookbook of recipes by mystery/thriller writers *Sleuth Stew*. I am very grateful to the editors of *Has-Beens on Parade* for this opportunity to share these reminiscences from my early career. I know that many people would be offended at being solicited by such a fanzine, but I am not in total denial on my lack of writing success, and I feel that my work in *WINT* is one of the most satisfying of my life.

First let me tell you a little about myself. Not that I was born and so forth, you probably have a good idea about that, no I want to explain the late twentieth century to you. Everyone wanted to be a writer, because a good deal of effort in the craft seemed to have been removed. My mother had told me with horror that in her first job she had a manual typewriter. It was one of those tales of "how bad it was" that ranked up there with the idea of a TV without remote control. There were all kinds of software in those days that helped you write. They formatted the text, they prompted you with both words and plot, and they even encouraged you if you stopped writing due to some from of block. I remember when the first time my computer got the (as it was then called) World Wide Web. It was as much of a breakthrough then as doing away with keyboards had been a few years before.

My job[1] or as we said then, my job, was a manager of a video store in Austin, Texas. It was the "cool" video store next to New Atlantis, which was a used bookstore, and a bar called the Decline of West. It didn't pay for shit, but it did bring in a steady group of artistic people. Austin was sort of a writers' colony in those days. You couldn't spit without hitting a published author. I know because I spit a lot, mainly just at the people walking by into Violet Crown Videos. My girlfriend worked for me and made even less. We considered ourselves to be as cool as our videos. But we had one tragic secret. Unlike our clientele, we hadn't achieved in any art form. Now we were smart enough to see writers don't have any money, or they wouldn't have grumbled so at the dollar a day late fee on their DVD's (I'm guessing that the readership of *HBOP* is historically savvy enough to pick up on most of my quaint terms. If they ain't that's too bad because I'm not being paid for this). But everyone was working on something. Neal, the stock boy, was working on a screenplay, Susan on her novel and Tagi on an opera. Belinda, my girlfriend, had done some painting that we used to fix a whole in the roof of our garage. I had learned to play "Stairway to Heaven" on the guitar, and even worked in a band that got to play at a couple of parties, until some drunk guy threw our drummer into the river. But we began to get the wannabe spirit.

How tough could writing be? After all, New Atlantis was filled with it, clearly most of it turned out by people less smart than us, if not in fact less talented. I asked Mary Denning, a founder of the Contrarians, a school of Austin writers, what her secret was. "Persistence." She said. I figured I could try that awhile, at least until it got boring. Picking what to write was the next hurdle. I asked all the writers that came in, what sold, and they all said mysteries. So I got some mystery writing software, and I took off. My first novel was entitled *The Woman with Three Breasts.* I thought my grand climax was stunning, "She gazed horrified at one of three breasts. *It was made of wax."* It took me months to write and despite my sending it to three or four publishers I couldn't sell it. Therefore, I decided to try my hand at short fiction. That way I wouldn't spend so long at creating the thing.

Meantime Belinda was trying a more social approach she had joined a group of people that wanted to write mysteries called People Who Want to Write Mysteries (PWWtWM) or as they affectionately called it, "Pootem," The group brought famous people in the field of mystery writing to Austin—agents and publishers and such—which would surely snap up some of the locally produced delicacies. So we both attended and shelled out money for workshops. We watched other people being published left and right. In fact at out first workshop the woman who had set to the left of me and the man who had sat to the right of me, both sold a mystery novel in a month.

Was there some cosmic conspiracy against us?

I wrote many short stories in those days," The Dairy Queen Murders," "The Jell-O Slayer," "The Pork and Bean Menace." But none of them sold. One was even returned to me with a thin pencil scrawl "It's the food guy again." I would show them. I tired writing about drinks.

About this time Horace Greenslau came on the scene. Horace appeared in the form of unsolicited e-mail (or as we called in those halcyon days "Spam.") Horace presented him self to the brethren and cistern of Pootem as a wily old publisher with many tricks up his ink stained sleeves. He pointed out two facts. Fact number one: the second sale is easier to make than the first, so if you want to be a published author, the best thing you can be is already published. Fact number two: you don't have to pay dead guys anything but respect. His emails to Pootem just talked about these ideas, he said he just kept thinking about them.

So one day I sent a note to this list saying why not put them together? You could put a book that was half stuff by dead guys that you didn't have to pay any money to, and half by living guys that were first time writers.

What a great idea! Wrote Greenslau.

It became his project at once. He had spots for eleven writers, to mixed with eleven classics of detection. It would be called *Mystery Classics*. He had some has-been guy, D. B. Bowen, author of *The Cellophane Fawn Trilogy*, on hand to write an intro for five hindered smackers. He would mention the twenty tales one by one and thus give illusion that the new guys ranked up there with Chandler, Borges, Doyle, and so forth. The classics were great from literary to hard-boiled, impressionistic to great logic tales. There was only one rub.

Money.

He didn't want to do it as a vanity press, no that was evil. He simply needed each of his writers to buy—say—two hundred copies. They could easily sell them to libraries, specialty shops, their friends and relatives. What proud momma wouldn't buy a book that listed her baby son after Agatha Christie? He would sell the rest.

I know what you are thinking. Well it's easy to think things like that when fame isn't around the corner and some guy is telling you that can sell two hundred books.

Belinda and I figured it this way. I could put a display of the books for sake at the store, plus I could take a suitcase full of them to our family reunions, then when the store sold off its used videos at the flea market in the spring I could sell a few more copies then. Before long we could sell our four hundred.

So we coughed up the cash and we wrote out tales. Mine was "The Butcher Wore Red" and hers was "The Video Store Murders." Nine other people in Pootem likewise coughed up the cash.

The books took a long time to materialize. Since we had never met him in the flesh, we began to wonder if we had been scammed.

When the books did show up, they were as nicely produced as we had imagined for the rather hefty price we had put out. Belinda and I had visualized them as leather bound with gilt lettering and quaint illustrations (at least for the real classics). Greenslau had also asked each of us for a black-and-white photo. I guess he had merely asked for his collection, there weren't any picture in the book.

Bowen's introduction was little weird too. He had very perceptive things about the classic tales, but made fun of us. For example, "In Moses Gubb's 'The Bucher Wore Red' we see an interesting attempt to turn a food obsession into a tale of detection. Although the astute reader will have guessed the identity of the killer long before the end of the tale, his obsessive writing will have a special appeal for a certain type of reader interested in the workings of the authorial mind." Sad to say, mine was not the worst.

But it was a book. It had an ISBN number. It, for the most part, spelled out names right, and it was a **hardback**, not something easily recycled. It would live on in libraries and bookshelves of our friends.

To my surprise and initial glee, I was listed as the editor. Greenslau had sent a note when everyone's book was delivered reminding him or her it had been my idea.

The local paper reviewed us. The reviewer liked all the things the dead people had written. It called the editor "only half bad."

Our relatives did buy copies. But our friends couldn't afford them. Local specialty shops like Adventures in Crime and Space were willing to buy a couple, but the look of pity in the eyes of the owner didn't make us feel very good.

You know, nobody buys expensive anthologies at

flea markets. But some people did ask us on advice on how to get published. Then I started getting little nasty notes from my fellow authors. They had all laid out nearly three thousand dollars apparently for the purpose of loosing closet space. Nobody blamed Greenslau; everyone remembered that I had thought it up. Your most noble moments may be like the seeds of a dandelion, but e-mail lives forever. (Well at least it did in those uncivilized days).

A year passed. We did our best to sell copies. One of our members a dentist did sell his off to his clients, but he offered them a price break on his services. The few books we gave away as review copies showed up in used bookstores around town, anchors in the cheap bins. I lost my friends in the group. I lost Belinda for other reasons, but when she left me her copies of the book stayed in the garage. Fine. I made a pile of them and propped up a roof beam.

I became guilty. I felt that it was my fault. The least I could do was buy up the cheap copies of the books around town. They usually went for one or two bucks. I made a game of it, wearing dark glasses and pulling a hat over my face, I would go out and bag a few on nights of the new moon.

I don't know how many copies I had bought before I discovered that there were variant editions of *Mystery Classics*. One night I opened one up. There were tales by the eleven masters and eleven people I had never heard of. There was an introduction by D. B. Bowen for eleven writers—all of whom lived in Houston, Texas.

So I went out in my garage. The books looked the same on the outside, but close inspection soon reveled that I owned the Santa Fe, Dallas, and Anchorage versions of *Mystery Classics*. I drove to the copy shop and began shooting copies of the alternate title pages. Each edition had its own editor, some fall guy (or in the case of Anchorage fall gal) that had had the same "brilliant" idea that I had had. I spent all night addressing envelopes. I wanted all the Austin writers to know. To know that I hadn't done it. To know that somewhere Mr. Greenslau was traveling from town to town raking the dough from would be writers. I had to use snail mail; they wouldn't take my calls anymore.

At first my fellow writers weren't concerned. Most of them apologized to me. We talked a little about contacting the other victims, but mainly we were embarrassed. Most of us had had friends that had warned us that the whole thing smelled like a scam, and we were embarrassed. But Belinda changed all that. She set up a mailing list for us all and she wrote a really impassioned letter about how I had been screwed over. She told them that I had paid for her books, and that I had bought all the copies, and that I had taken all their abuse (including hers), and that I had let them know what had happened. She was really mad at Greenslau, and when people realized that I was out over six thousand dollars, they got mad to.

I think it was Dr. Ellison, the dentist, who suggested that we should get our revenge. We agreed early on but we didn't know how.

Belinda began researching the place that had printed all the books it was in Polk City, Iowa. Other than printing *Mystery Classics*, they did Bibles in Spanish and menus. Their equipment was old, and the *CM* line kept them going. They were very friendly, and were glad to give her a list of cities that had had *CM*s made up. We looked it over. Greenslau had neglected New Orleans. We couldn't guess why, maybe he thought the bunco squad there was too good. So we got a local ISP and we made a group Crescent City Crime Writers. We got us a webpage, we took out some ads in the *New Orleans Picayune*, and we mentioned our name on a few mystery news groups. We had people that wanted to join of course, but we told them that we had already filled our meeting space—some unspecified loft on Canal Street and that it would be a while before we were taking members, but they were free to chat. We adopted pseudonyms, we chatted, and we even learned some things about the city of New Orleans and its rich mystery tradition. Eventually someone made the observation that it is sure to easy to get published if you already are published. His name was Reds law. Mr.Redslaw went on to tell us that the reasons dead guys are reprinted is that they sell and you don't have to pay them.

Therefore, I went on-line as Mr. Phineas Thibodaux, an honest but poor man of the parishes with a great marketing strategy....

Mr. Redslaw thought my notion of an anthology of half classic and half virgin talent was nothing short of genius. He said he could get a has-been writer, a Mr. D. B. Bowen, author of *The Cellophane Trilogy*, would write an introduction.

Here is where we made our move. We said that we wanted to meet him, Mr. Bowen, of course. We had figured out that much.

At first there was reluctance. Redslaw told us that Bowen was reclusive, alcoholic, etc. We stuck to our guns, and Belinda had a brilliant idea. She researched Bowen. He had written five avant-garde novels in the eighties. The *CTT* had been marginally successful. He had been on the list of several critics as **the** young writer to watch. He had speaking tours, was a minor TV celeb, but each novel got stranger and the readership declined. He even tried vanity publishing with—you guessed it—the Menu House in Polk City.

So in addition to our wanting to see him, we began to say good things about his work.

There isn't the writer alive that doesn't believe flattery. The entire strange cursed race thinks that someday their scribblings will have a place in god's eternal bookshelf.

Our plan was a little vague. We thought that we get him in a hotel room and then just confront him and in some magical way he would pay us back the money he had sucked away.

We choose an older hotel in the French Quarter called the Roosevelt. We rented the big penthouse that had looked over Mardi-gras for almost a hundred years. It was bleak December. We told him to meet us at eight on a Wednesday night. We dressed well, and those of us who had concealed weapons permits from Texas were packing. We had no intention of killing him, just scaring him into the straight and narrow.

Belinda had a tape recorder so we could catch any confessions that might boil to the surface.

He was fifteen minutes late. We were sweating and uncomfortable. We heard the old elevator make its way to our floor. Belinda and a woman named Chandra Lee escorted him to our suite. He was older and thinner than we had thought. We had our chairs arranged in a circle, his was in the middle. He laughed when he saw it. We guessed he wouldn't be laughing soon.

After he had set down, we all reached under our chairs and pulled out a copy of *Mystery Classics*, except for me I pulled our five copies—one of each of the editions I had bought. We were expecting fear or guilt.

We were disappointed.

He just asked, "So which group are you? Shreveport? Dallas? No I guess it's too long for it to be Dallas."

I said, "We're Austin and we want our money back."

"Oh that's original," he said, relaxing in his chair, "About as original as your fiction." Then he laughed.

"Look Bowen, we're not fooling around." Said Dr. Ellison.

"Of course you are," said Bowen, "That's all you've ever done. You're jerk-offs. What do you want from me? You said you wanted to be published. Well you got your book. It's big, it's fat. I bought all of you have discovered the great utility it has for propping things up. You should be as happy as a pig in slop. But no, what you wanted wasn't to pay three thousand dollars so that your useless names would be printed along side people that would sneer at your ineptitude. But you wanted more. You are disappointed that I am not Satan. You wanted to sell your souls for fame. Well, you don't have soul, or you could have written something worthwhile. You don't got shit."

"No Bowen," I said, "We've got you."

"You think your first the group that has pieced this together. You're not, and you're not the last. But everything I did was legal. I knew this was a confrontation when I walked down here. Night meeting in an old hotel in the French Quarter, the same old clichéd stuff that keep your fiction from selling. I just wanted to see your pathetic faces, look at you, all dressed up, all proper; does it make you feel powerful? Your little chairs all in a circle. Well I'm going now, and you can go back to your lives and tiny dreams."

"Do you think you are a good writer, Bowen?"

"I'm no Rex Hull, but I'm OK. I'm third-rate, but my ambition is too great. So I look for eighteenth-rate scum to support me."

He rose.

"No." said Dr. Ellison, "We are not done with you."

"Why what are you going to do kill me?"

"Yes." Dr. Ellison said, "We are. Just because you aren't expecting it. It is a sign of the triumph of our poor imaginations.

We were on him in a minute. Eleven people can over power a man in his sixties easily. Killing him is easier still.

Taking a corpse through the French Quarter is not a difficult matter when he is small. You simply stand on either side of him and tell on-lookers that he has too much to drink. In fact as we took him to my car, we passed another fellow in the same straights. Perhaps he too was dead.

We took him to my cousin's restaurant. We sat outside until closing time. My cousin and I had an agreement. He did not ask about things that he didn't want to hear the answer to, and I treated his life the same way.

We made Mr. D. B. Bowen into jambalaya. The other men butchered him, while I prolapsed the rice and sauce as per the recipe in my story. He was ready at dawn, and we filled up our containers with him and took him to our homes in Austin. Just before we took off, Belinda said, "Well he's toast now." I most emphatically denied that he was toast, and took offences at the slighting of my culinary creation. "OK," she said, "He is not toast."

We were prepared to be each other's alibis when the law came by.

It never came.

Bowen did live alone. He was the alcoholic recluse he claimed to be. Eventually the residence hotel he lived in Washington must have noticed that their tenant had not returned.

The others had swore off writing, but I turned out

a few tales afterward—some of which sold. I felt my fiction getting better, and attributed it to some endorphin released after revenge.

About six months later, Belinda was listening to Bowen's speech in the Roosevelt Penthouse. She called me and said that it was very dramatic. The whole thing would make a lovely crime novel. So we broke it into eleven chapters. Each of us did our best. And unlike most of our scribbling before and after, our best was finally good enough. Sure the novel sold as something of a curiosity like *Naked Came the Spy*, but it did sell. We had a few minutes of fame—woefully short of the fifteen minutes that a man named Andy Warhol had promised our parent's generation.

The success of the book, plus my modest sales before its publication inspired everyone to try writing again. We had all felt the writing we did on *WINT* had been smooth and beautiful. We were all able to get agents on the strengths of *WINT*'s sales, and we were busy turning out novel proposals. But something was wrong.

The quality left our writing. At first we hid this each from the other. All right at first we hid it form ourselves, a writer cannot bear to acknowledge that his best days may be gone—especially if his best days were about a month in length. However, by the time the movie of *WINT* came out, our writing was as bad as it had been in *Mystery Classics*; we didn't know what had happened. Had the crime been enough to stimulate our moribund muses?

Dr. Ellison suggested a different explanation.

Over half a century before, certain experiments on planaria learning had suggested that cannibalism lead to the exchange of knowledge. The planaria, a type of flatworm, were tested with a maze and their times recorded. Then the planaria were ground up and fed to a new generation, who could solve the maze in less time than their predecessors. It was speculated that their was a transference of knowledge—probably in the messenger RNA strands of the planaria The experiment was later discredited, as some researched believed that the mazes were contaminated by the smell of the flatworm's passage and that was the guiding force. However, certain people believed that the experiments were discredited to keep universities form turning into professor-hamburger stands.

*Hoc est corpus meum.*

Maybe we had eaten Bowen's talent. Unlike him we were not jaded nor overcome by a desire to be known in a limited genre—we were just people with a burning desire to write, but perhaps nothing to say. Our desire plus his RNA got one more novel out of him. It was sad that he never got the fame, which he like us, had craved. The RNA material must have peaked in us about nine months after the deed and receded nine months afterward.

Our reaction to Dr. Ellison's theory varied. Some of us were glad at our one shot at fame and parlayed into little victories like my cookbook. Others drank themselves to death like Belinda, who could face the fact she had no talent. Of course the best known case—

the one you've been reading this interview to see if I would mention—see I still have a few mystery writer tricks even if I am eighteenth-rate—was Dr. Ellison. One of the good dentist's clients was Vernon Ghosh, a well-know writer of techno-thrillers. Ellison gassed him when he was in for his yearly dental visit and then cut up his body with an eye to making lasagna from it. The unfortunate visit of a young mad with a chipped tooth exposed Ellison's attempt at cannibalism.

Ironically it lead to new interest in our work and a re-release of *WINT*, which has remained in print since. We all denied any understanding of his actions, and if in our black hearts we had been thinking of a similar deed, we abandoned such evils schemes.

Although not quite the youngest of our little group of wannabes I am the last to draw breath, and I will not do so for much longer. I enjoyed sharing our story for *Has-Beens on Parade*.

# DIARY FOUND IN AN ABANDONED STUDIO

I couldn't paint when I took the medicine.

If I laid off for a few days the images would come and I could finish a canvas, but there was always the danger that I would forget who was doing the painting, or maybe even right and wrong. So I started this diary. I'll read it every day and write in it every day and that way I won't get in trouble like that other time. Yesterday I prepared a canvas. Today I put my medicine aside. Tomorrow I'll start my sketches.

Day 2. My name is Tyrone Watson. I am thirty-eight. I live in Austin, Texas. There that seems pretty sane. I don't think it's a good idea to kill one's critics. Violence has no special beauty. If I want to get people, I'll just caricature them. I work for Roberta Sais.

I started today on *The Market of Values*, which will be a study in blues and grays of people at some sort of carnival buying and selling things of no value. Maybe I'll work in miniatures of Bessie Vollman's paintings.

Day 3. Ideas are getting really slippery today. It feels great. My sketchbook is filling up and *Market*s coming along. Oh I forgot to do my focusing mantra.

My name is Tyrone Watson, MFA. I have had two one-man exhibitions. The last was five years ago.

There that's in control. In fact the only control problem I have is wanting to spend all my time up here painting instead of down in the shop, but that's normal. Artists want to do art. It's a pity that business hours coincide with the light being good.

Day 4. Depressed today.

Day 5. Depressed today. Did nothing. Got mad.

Day 6. My name is Tyrone Watson. I am thirty-eight. I live in Austin. I had a great day. A Mr. Simon Pound had a lot to ask me about my art. Maybe I'm in for a comeback. I started to take him upstairs and show him my work in progress, but a little voice told me not to. I don't mean a little voice like before, I just mean a hunch, that feeling of not letting people in on it until you're ready. I got a lot done today. *Market* should be finished tomorrow.

Day 7. Finished *Market*. Not as good as I had hoped, but still that's the essence of the artistic personality. Always dissatisfied. Like Faust. I'm starting something more free form, a response to those people who caused me so much trouble. I'm going to call it *Exposed Heart*. I'm not sure how to start. Well an idea suggests itself, but not a good one. My name is Tyrone Watson. I'm thirty something a painter on the go.

Day 8. Busy.

Day 9. Spent several hours with my model.

Day 10. Mr. Pound came by today. I was disappointed to learn he wasn't an art critic. He is a retired cop. His life story seemed pretty interesting. Maybe I'll do him after *Exposed Heart* which is coming along nicely thank you. It's a little bit more gory than anything I've done in years.

Day 11. My name is Tyrone Watson. Today Mr. Pound came by and we discussed our life stories, which were amazingly similar. I want to get to know him because I'm going to do a picture of him called *The Multidimensional Blue Lines* .

He became a cop in the '70s. His big ambition from the first was to make detective. He studied every text on criminology, took every possible course and dedicated his ife to that particular transformation, but various political forces downtown saw to it that he didn't make the grade.

I told him how critics had ruined my two shows, particularly the second show when Bessie Vollman's competing exhibition won such lavish praise. She had been the more "politically correct" artist. So her career took off and I managed a used bookstore for minimum wage and free studio space.

He asked if he could see my work in progress, and I told him no. I hate anyone to see something before I'm done with it. But I told him that I was interested in painting him. At first he seemed surprised, then readily agreed.

He asked me if I knew anything about the death of two art critics five years ago.

I asked him if he was still a cop.

He said that he quit the force a couple of years ago.

He'd arrested too many criminals who got off on technicalities. So he quit. He was near enough retirement anyway and he had a few investments that had paid off well. He liked to keep his hand in. The police, he assured me, at least the good cops—the real force—still called him for advice.

I asked him how long he'd been interested in art. He said that every good cop is interested in art. The artistic mind and the criminal mind are very, very similar. Most criminals, he reasoned, were failed artists.

But criminals don't have critics, I told him.

"Of course they do," he said. "Cops, they catch inept criminals. The great criminals go free."

I had never thought of a cop as a critic for a criminal's art.

Day 12. Terrible dreams last night. I was too depressed to open the store.

Day 13. It's been almost two weeks and I'm doing fine. Maybe I'm over my trouble. My name is Tyrone Watson. Elementary, my dear Watson. Someone broke into the shop last night, they didn't take anything but I think they may have been through my studio. Both the outside door and the studio door were open. Despite this I can't tell you how GREAT I feel. I started two different paintings this morning. I started to call the owner and tell her the shop had been broken into, but realized that would screw up my process. I painted like Picasso. I'll stay here at night. Maybe I'll catch my burglar and paint him. I'm ready. I'm ready for anything. I feel GREAT!

Day 14. I painted well into the night and finished my first painting; a riotous and much spangled study in purple and green called *The Water People Are Talking to Me*. I went out for a walk about 3:00 AM. I needed inspiration for the second piece—a study in chrome yellow called *Voltman Discharges*. Oh what a wonderful great buzzy great picture! Zip zzp, I say, zip zap.

Day 15. Mr. Pound came by with the news about Bessie Vollman. I felt really, really bad for a moment as though it had something to do with me. I suppose that shows I have a great soul that I can feel sorry for a rival. I asked to see the obituary notice since he was carrying the paper. Sure enough although I was Bessie's greatest rival I wasn't mentioned. Maybe I should send a wreath or something, after all I would be remembered a hundred years hence and she will be forgotten. Maybe I should go to the funeral to do a second painting of her.

Mr. Pound told me that he was unable to find any references to my one-man show five years ago. He said he was hoping to see some photos of my previous work. He seemed genuinely sad when I told him that it had all been purchased by Japanese investors.

Did I have unsold pieces that I might consider parting with?

Of course I had to tell him that I sold everything a few years ago when devastating poverty took hold of my life.

We all have our ups and downs, he said. He is truly

a wise man for a cop.

I asked him when he would come sit for me and he became agitated. I guess the thought of sitting for eternity is frightening to some. It brings out that fear that their flaws, that one tiny flaw that everybody has, might bemagnified through the ages. After awhile all they would be would be the flaw.

My name is Vincent van Gogh and I'm one hundred and thirty-eight years old. Just kidding.

Day 16. I dreamt I was a child again. It must've been when I was in the sixth grade. We had an art teacher who we went to see twice a week. She gave us the assignment of drawing something on the school yard, so I drew the blue portable toilets that had been placed on the football field. I could see them from my desk if I craned my neck over. The bell rings and class is over and I was supposed to have the picture finished by the end of the period. Mrs. Elgood came over and told me to give it to her. That I could work on it Thursday. I said just a minute I could finish it and then it was done and I handed it to her, and she said, "Tyrone, there is nothing like this outside." I told her to look and she wouldn't look and I told her to look and she wouldn't look so I took hold of her head and tried to make her look and I pushed her face through the glass and she bled.

Then I woke up and all I can say is you should have looked.

I re-read my entry for yesterday. I am really mad that the newspaper files have been tampered with. Maybe

I'll go paint all of them. I'll paint every fucking critic into a corner. I was too mad to open the shop today. I heard some people knocking and the damn phone kept ringing. Ring a ding a ding until I took it off the hook. Probably the damn owner. I'll take care of her too. You shouldn't disturb a genius at work. There should be a law. I painted a bright red and orange painting today *Angry Sun Bites Man*. I'll open up tomorrow.

Day 17. Depressed and mad.

Day 18. The police banged and banged on my door. Mr. Pound wasn't with them. They wanted to know if I knew that Ms. Roberta Sais, who owned the Book Cellar (and who in theory is my employer) had died. No, I said, I didn't know. Murdered, they said. No, I said, I didn't know. I was very busy. I had to work on my paintings. I thanked them for the news. She had heirs, they said. I said I always thought she put on airs. Heirs, they said, I should close the shop until the heirs came. And I said good. I made a "Closed on Account of Death" sign and hung it in the door.

In the afternoon Mr. Pound came by and pounded on my door until I answered it. I told him we were closed.

He said he was here to pose.

I let him in to do some sketches. He started to go up stairs to my studio. I told him I do my sketches in the shop. He wasn't easy to sketch because he kept talking. He hinted that he was a vigilante going after criminals the system might let off on some technicality—like no Miranda rights. Lots of stories of cars in the nights. For some reason I pictured them as moving silently and without headlights. "Dark of night doesn't stop you, eh?" I asked.

He reacted violently, then chuckled, and said, "No dark of night doesn't stop me."

He talked a lot about criminals who made their confessions got off easily. With his pull down at the station he could help such a criminal. If the criminal doing the murders now were, say, to confess to him, he could make it very easy on the guy.

If on the other hand the current murderer were to try to weasel out—to escape from the long arm of the law—he would make it very difficult for him. He would track the murderer down and strike when the killer least expected it.

He didn't ask to see my sketches, which was good, because I wasn't pleased with them. When I left I tore them all up in little pieces.

I am going to sleep in the studio tonight—to protect my paintings. I am worried about them somehow.

Day 19. Today I painted *The Last Innocent Man*. The picture is full of big blue eyes looking everywhere. In the lower right corner is a single yellow square—representing a window. Inside an artist can be seen painting a flowery peaceful landscape. I may change the title to *This Is My Skull*.

Day 20. This morning I came to my senses and took my medicine. I realized I must have done some pretty bad things. I figured I'd wait for Mr. Pound, and when he came I'd confess to him. He could make it easy for me. He was my friend. I waited all day, but he didn't show.

About six I called the downtown police station. Mr. Pound had told me that he still had friends on the force. I figured I could ask around and they could put me in touch with him. It took forever to get in touch with homicide. While I waited I cursed myself for not having got his number. Then I got Detective Blick. I asked if he knew Mr. Pound.

"Mr. Clarence Pound?" he asked.

"I'm not sure of his first name. He is a retired policeman. He had told me he still had friends on the force."

"Let me guess, he told you that he tried to make detective but 'political' forces kept him from making the grade. He also said that he was a vigilante, bringing criminals to justice who had escaped their just desserts."

"Well, yes," I said.

"I am sorry to tell you this, sir, but Clarence Pound is a retired postal worker with some severe personality problems. Every few months he stops his medication for awhile and gets to thinking he's some super-cop. If he's been bothering you, let me know and we'll pick him up and take him to his doctor."

"No. He hasn't been bothering me at all. Thank you."

I hung up as he was asking "Who are—"

Mr. Pound is some kind of nut. I'll have to be ready for him.

Day 21. I slept in the studio and he broke in. I woke up and saw him looking at my paintings. He had a gun in one hand and a flashlight in the other.

"They're blank," he said. "All of these canvasses just painted white."

"No," I said, "They're very subtle. You must study them carefully."

"They're blank. You're some kind of nut."

"No, you're the nut. You're an ex-postal employee. You're not a cop. You've never been a cop."

"That's not true." He pointed the gun at me.

"It is true. You're not a cop."

Suddenly he sat down. Just sort of collapsed. He didn't say anything for a long time. I thought about going over and taking his gun away.

Then he began to talk in a low monotone. He explained who he really was and everything became clear to me.

He is Mr. Carlos Pound, owner of a very important gallery in New York. Today we are putting my paintings into a U-Haul van. We will drive up to New York, where he'll host a one-man show for me.

I bet we make quite a splash.

# THE THIRTYERS

When the world didn't end in the Year 2000, the Reverend Jessie Cancun was among the first people to proclaim the idea of the "Babylon Calendar." According to Rev. Cancun, the evil forces of the Whore of Babylon had stolen the right and true calendar of the pious and replaced it in the year 1066, which was actually 1096. It was unclear to the general public why Rev. Cancun had taken the year of the Norman Conquest as the pivotal moment for the calendar hoax by the forces of Darkness. His own explanation that "1096 adds up to 16, whereas 1066 adds up to 13," while numerically true (if there is some **reason** for such addition of constitute digits), seemed at best a bit odd. The same could be said of 904 and 934 for example. But Rev. Cancun did little to woo the public.

Yet his church, the Grand Convocation of the Missing Thirty, otherwise known as the Thirtyers, did not lack for members. Many, many people had been involved in one belief system or another that had seen great change as likely in 2000, if not indeed the very End of the World. And the great Psychic Depression of the Oughties contributed to his membership.

The basic tenets of the faith were five. First, the real End of the World would happen in 2030 (or, as they reckoned it, 2000). Second, the faithful needed to gather in a community that banned the evil Babylon calendar. Third, the consumption of fast foods was evil. Fourth, the taking of new names after tourist paradises was necessary—the Rev. Cancun's birth name had been Trexler. Fifth, the avoidance of the World Wide Web, which had distracted all of us by promoting the myth of Babylon 2000, and thus tricking people out of the real End of the World. The odd nature of the beliefs (especially the tourist name-taking) gave the cult a good deal of publicity in the early Oughties. Both Rev. Cancun and his sister the Rev. Waikiki were interviewed great deal in those days, and although they avoided the WWW with great fear and loathing, a number of pages were kept **about** them.

But as the Psychic Renaissance of the Teens started such oddball faiths were usually forgotten, since by and large mankind had better things to do. The lure of the weird is always with us however and as the Babylon Calendar approached 2029, my editor wanted me to research the Thirtyers—see if any of them still hung on to the faith, how did they live, what were their fears at the coming millennium.

Information on the sect was very limited. The older pieces written decades before were easy to find in the GreatData Snowball, but nothing appeared after 2012. They had bought a small town in Oklahoma, the site of a bankrupt ashram. They had renamed their community 2X15, pronounced "Two ex Fifteen" apparently a private joke on Y2K, which my readers may remember as the buzzword used to describe the Millennium. Their desire to be cut off from the increasingly integrated WWW meant that didn't even have phones or cable television. They didn't even allow cars into their town, according to the 2012 article. I couldn't rightly think of any appliance that wasn't connected to the WWW. Could you imagine not being able to ask your refrigerator if it had ordered those carrots you like? They must live in a weird pre-animist world, thoroughly unlike the one we live in.

I decided to go there.

I had to find a horse, a real unmodified horse. But it was Oklahoma, after all.

The nearest town was Gilliam, Oklahoma, and nobody there knew anything about 2X15. "Nobody goes there. I think they all died or moved out a long time ago."

I had to fully insure the horse. I was, after all, leaving to a new and unknown realm where people might keep time with knotted cords and slay one another with stone axes. I hoped that the folks of 2X15 hadn't kept up with the ways of Babylon so they wouldn't know that I had been modified, as at least half the world was.

I had downloaded some files on horse riding, and I set off for the West. I had assumed that my satellite links would be active all the way there. I mean, the satellite net covers Africa and Asia and Antarctica— so I figured that Oklahoma was a sure thing.

So when the comforting voices began to fade out a few miles from the village, I was scared. I was going to be alone. I hadn't been alone since I was seven or eight years old. I started to panic, and the horse, a chestnut gelding, felt my fear.

He galloped a little wildly, and I let out a scream. I almost fell, but grabbing the reins and concentrating on bringing the beast under control calmed me. When my horse stopped, all was quiet. I couldn't will a message to anyone. I couldn't ask for a map. I didn't even know what time it was.

Have you ever not known what time it was?

Even unmodified humans have only to ask that question out loud, and something will answer—whether it is a coffee pot or their shoes.

I was in a different world. The primitive world.

This would make a great story.

I imagined billions of people downloading it.

I spurred my horse and we headed for the village of 2X15. It took me a moment to realize that the outer world was quiet as well. There were birds and insects, but no machines. As I approached the village, there were no animals. This puzzled me. I had read Rev. Waikiki's diatribes against fast food, which any sane person would agree with now after the Burger Wars of the Twenties, but I had never seen any avocation of vegetarianism. Perhaps the cult had left the area—but how did they jam the satellite system? It could be that they had some arrangements with the folks running the system, but surely I would have found that in my researches.

When the village came in view, there was no movement on the streets, but the hanging corpses swayed in the wind.

Most light posts, trees, and flagpoles held a corpse. In other places the ropes had rotted or frayed and dumped their cargo at the base of the pole. My horse didn't like this and whinnied with fear. I didn't like it either, but I tied him to a tree outside of the village limits.

The road sign still stood. **2X15 No Babylon Time, No Babylon Channels Under Penalty of Death**.

My first and biggest concern was that whoever had done the hangings was still around, but I saw that most of them had been hanged a long time. I immediately asked for information about corpses, and chills ran up my spine when no voice filled my head. I was truly in the Land of the Dead.

Some of the corpses were small. Children.

I walked into the town. There was a little square parking the center, overgrown and full of the oldest corpses—all mere skeletons at the base of trees, grass growing lush in their rib cages. Here is where the hangings must have started. The asphalt in the streets was rubble, and time (or some other mischievous agent) had broken many windows in the buildings.

Nothing was clearly the center of government, but there was an old post office on one side of the square. I went unhopefully, looking for some sign of what madness had over-taken the village.

The post office smelled very, very foul when I

opened the doors. I realized then, that I hadn't smelled anything from the corpses.

There wasn't any light. I didn't see any torches or kerosene lanterns, so I surmised that the Thirtyers had used electricity that they had generated somehow, but no one maintained the power plants any longer.

The windows were dirty, but there was enough light to see a strange statue behind the counter of an old man standing as though he were Atlas holding up the world. In front of the statue was a big book, a ledger of some sort filled with entries too cribbed to read in the dim light. I picked it up and took it outside.

They were names.

And crimes.

Randolph Riviera. Television.

Susan Las Vegas. Telephone.

Sharon Aspen. Data Download.

The first entries were written in a very legible handwriting, with dates (all thirty years too soon). But the handwriting got too large and more than a little shaky.

On the last page, I read the following.

Mary Waikiki. Vanity Search on Web 1999.

I am alone now. I can't fight the urge to hold off my desire to speak. It is only a few months. I must be stronger. I must hold the world at bay. I must see in the Millennium.

I realized what the statue was, and I ran in.

"Rev. Cancun?" I asked.

The weird figure stirred a little.

"Can't talk to anyone," he said.

Than it/he tumbled forward. Suddenly my mind was filled with quiet prompts from the world-wide information system. I sent off a request for a medic, but they were too late. The Rev. Cancun had held off the world by will alone, stronger, in the end, than his flock, who had to turn to TV, and WWW, and other news. He came within two months of his 2000, and now he lives on as the most popular story of 2029.

# ABOUT THE AUTHOR

**DON WEBB** was born in 1960 in Amarillo, Texas. His works range from a St. Martin Press mystery series, to poetry, and fiction and nonfiction books on the occult. He attended Rice University and the University of Texas at Austin. Don is the poster child of literary ADHD. He's written a rock-'n'-roll song for French radio, the I-phone App "Office Ching," and has done game design for FASA and TSR. He's also penned a lot of horror stories. His mom says that Don is her favorite horror writer—after Ramsey Campbell! He's been translated into twelve languages; ten of his poems have been published in Chinese in *Selected Poems of Post-Beat Poets*.

He lives in Austin, Texas, with his lovely wife Guiniviere and their cats Big Pig and Sascha. He cries at the sight of bluebonnets in the spring, the ending of the *Whole Wide World*, and losses of the Longhorn football team.

www.ingramcontent.com/pod-product-compliance
Lightning Source LLC
Chambersburg PA
CBHW031403250626
47155CB00004B/1392

# GARGOYLE NIGHTS

In the last days of Oldearth's greatest city, a powerful sorcerer seeks eternal life, but in the process creates a monster of fearsome evil and dire terror—The Gargoyle! This evil creature guards the dead of mystical Shenumbra, Earth's last city, millions of years in the future—when the old sun has grown cold, humanity is just a memory, and our weary world is set to expire.

Throughout these dark eons the Gargoyle has stood its lonely vigil over the fetid crypts and grim necropolis that once was the home of a long-dead race called man. Now, the star-traveling Leinites have come to this old dead planet to sack it in their relentless greed, seeking any treasure and forbidden knowledge that might be hidden there. Little do they realize, however, that they've set loose a horrendous being of primordial menace upon them all!

Borgo Press Books by GARY LOVISI

*Driving Hell's Highway: A Crime Novel*
*Gargoyle Nights: A Collection of Horror*
*Murder of a Bookman: A Bentley Hollow Collectibles*
  *Mystery Novel*

# GARGOYLE NIGHTS

## A COLLECTION OF HORROR

### GARY LOVISI

THE BORGO PRESS

MMXI

GARGOYLE NIGHTS

# DEDICATION

*For my young and lovely wife,*

## *Lucille*

# CONTENTS

# ACKNOWLEDGMENTS

THESE STORIES WERE previously published as follows, and are reprinted (with minor editing, updating, and textual modifications) by permission of the author:

"The Apothecarium of Yabool-Syn" was first published in the UK horror magazine, *Dagon*, issue #20, November, 1987. Copyright © 1987, 2011 by Gary Lovisi.

The three stories comprising this book were later published in the booklet, *The Gargoyle* by Gary Lovisi, Gryphon Books, 1988. They have been substantially revised for this special Borgo Press edition. Copyright © 1988, 2011 by Gary Lovisi.

# THE APOTHECARIUM
# OF YABOOL-SYN

# PART ONE
## AT THE MAGE'S DIRECTIVE

In the last days of Earth's last city, there lived a mage named Yabool-Syn, who was an apothecary of rare acumen and distinction; one astute in the culture of herbs and chemical contrivances, and whose vast knowledge of arcane enchantments and poultries was the talk of mystical Shenumbra.

Within his secluded manse, located in a section of the multi-tiered megalopolis known as the Eye of the Hellspoint, Yabool-Syn worked daily upon all manner of necromantic and magical directives.

His latest endeavor was a recreation of the wondrous Elixir of Life, a potion which would extend the gift of Foreverness to any brave enough to drink of this mysterious combination. However, to accomplish this vast feat the master magician needed one more ingredient to make a powerful composite of this arcane mixture, and obtaining that rare and missing item was what was turning the long hairs atop Yabool-Syn's head chalk gray at such an alarming rate. For the mage required a petal from the rare Rose of Exumanities, such a flower as does not even exist on this plane of Earthly delights,

but is native to more demon-haunted climes lost some-where in the nether dimensions between time, in a sub-strata of existence known as Topaz.

"I must have that last ingredient!" Yabool-Syn's voice boomed through his workroom lined with shelves full to the bursting point with time-weathered and hoary tomes containing the world's darkest secrets; and tables upon which all manner of strange devices, plants and animals resided. "And if I can not have it come to me—then I shall construct a golem of my own special manufacture and send it to travel the time lines to secure for me a sample of this most wondrous of floras."

So the master mage had decided upon a course of action and now he needed to create a likely surrogate of some effective manner to travel the planes of exis-tence and seek out his prize—for the master mage was not fool enough to go on such a mad and dangerous errand himself and thereby place his valuable persona in any number of terrible and unimagined dangers.

So Yabool-Syn thought hard upon what manner of creature was best suited for success in such an extreme and uncharted venture. Perhaps a human golem of the warrior variety? Or perhaps some horrible beastly servant? Mayhap some giant insecticide thing, or some empheral sprite from one of the nether realms? Well, he'd tried all of these and many others before—all without success. This time he decided he was in need of something quite different—and that was when his eyes fell upon the tiny mouse which lay sleeping in

yonder cage so peacefully oblivious to all the mighty troubles of the world.

And no sooner did the idea strike him than Yabool-Syn prepared a magnificent potion of Perambulative Sentience and force-fed the tiny and unwary rodent a dozen daring drops of the murkish liquid.

Well, the change in the tiny mouse was immediate and catastrophic, for Yabool-Syn knew that soon the creature's intelligence factor would be raised to such a level as to enable it to speak mind-to-mind, as many of the high lords of Shenumbra were able to converse amongst themselves and between such of the lesser beasts temporally raised to this exalted and lofty place of demi-godhood.

"My Lord, what have you done to me?" The mouse spoke with alarm and chattering fear at what had been done to him, words that went straight into the venerable mind of Yabool-Syn.

"I have need of your talents, little mouse, upon an errand of the utmost importance and complexity. Will you do as I instruct you? Your reward will be a hearty compensation."

Well, the mouse began to dwell upon this strange turn of events for a short time, carefully sniffing at the table he now found himself upon and at the air all around him. He curled his gorgeous tail and took a last long look back at what had been a rather grand cage, and then said with proper resignation, "I am but a small mouse and you are a great master here. I can do nothing but obey and trust you to keep your promise to

me after I have accomplished your desired deed."

"Very good. Spoken like a mouse among mice!" Yabool-Syn gloated with happy enthusiasm. Then he picked up the tiny rodent in careful hands and carried him to a cluttered work table where he placed him down, saying, "There is a place that I must send you now. It is an alien sphere, both dark and forbidding, but since you are a small and wary creature, you shall have little trouble and should survive all obstacles and dangers thrown your way. You will be going to a land called Topaz and you will be searching for a petal of the rare and wondrous Rose of Exumanities. When you find this rose call out to me. I will hear your voice echo through the spheres of time and bring you back safely to this reality. It is really all very simple. Do you not think so?"

The little mouse gauged his reply carefully. "Perhaps I am merely pessimistic in mind but with my new enhanced intelligence I seem to see all manner of problems could arise from this mission—not the least of which could be the possibility of considerable harm to my person," the tiny mouse said with most careful but polite insistence.

The mighty mage affected an annoyed look and then a slight shrug, "Oh, nonsense! I have taken great care to think of every alterative. That is why I am sending you in the first place, being a mouse you are the perfect creature to assure success in this venture. Now shed your pessimism and prepare for your greatest adventure!"

"Yes, of course, great mage, but what of the dangers?" the mouse asked with vaulted insistence. "Could not this rarest of roses be guarded by demon spawned things—huge felines with mouse-tasting claws?"

"All that I require of you is to snatch a petal of the rose and then call out to me. I will hear your voice and bring you back here safe and sound. Now what could be simpler than that?" Yabool-Syn told him with a twisted leer. Then his eyes bored down on the tiny mouse and his mind added in warning, "I think I need not elaborate to you the unpleasantries which will result should you invoke rescue without possessing a petal of the rose?"

"I see," the mouse said thoughtfully, recognizing the danger. "Well then, we had best proceed with this venture; for the sooner begun, the sooner ended, I say."

"Bravo Sir Mouse!" Yabool-Syn coached boldly as his optimism now burst forth. "I know now that I was right in choosing you for this most important mission. I congratulate you Mr. Mouse! Now, if you will allow me a moment to prepare things, I shall soon have you off into the other dimensional world of Topaz."

Well, the tiny mouse tried to look excited about his impending journey, it was after all an historic event for any rodent mouseling, but his artificially enhanced intelligence just persisted in showing him all manner of mammoth dangers—many with bright mouse-cutting claws and slavering lips that longed to feast upon tender mouse flesh. It is not a pleasant way to embark into the regions of the unknown at all.

Finally Yabool-Syn clapped his hands in wondrous delight and said, "Prepare yourself, my good mouse, for now all is in readiness and you beginning your greatest adventure!"

# PART TWO
## A MOUSE IN TOPAZ

Topaz is difficult to explain to one unaccustomed to the unique experience. In some manner it is merely a state of mind rather than a specific physical place, and yet it does have the form and substance of reality, with its own precarious existence being separate and distinct from other better-known and more worldly realities.

"So this is Topaz!" the tiny mouse thought to himself as he starred, wide-eyed at the many colors and shadows cascading around him as if dancing off the edge of the greatest of ancient waterfalls. It was a twisting and turning reality—where ground was up, and up was down, and the two could change perspective at any moment unbeknownst to a very tiny and confused mouse. A place where warmth and cold interchanged spontaneously to create wide divergences in atmosphere and temperature—snow that was burning to the flesh, rain that "fell" upwards, winds and doldrums existing in the same micro sphere, as well as negative gravity wells that caused the small rodent to float and flow, fly and flop about as if being buffeted by

an unknown hand.

"The Rose, my good mouse! Do not forget The Rose!" a powerful voice urged within his tiny skull, as the miniscule adventurer tried to orient his confused senses to the strangeness swirling about him so he could perform this most reluctant of missions and then return to the safety and security of his beloved cage.

The mouse surged forward being carried upon a morass of violent winds, through colors and bizarre imagination, eerie dreams and all manner of illusionary devices, until coming upon a great lumbering arbor that freely floated with many others in the mystical atmosphere—its monstrous roots streaming boldly outward—its great branches atop the other end growing in equally luxurious and wild abandon.

The little mouse was fascinated by the existence of these huge floating trees—and even more surprised when he noticed that which he saw growing so radiantly within the hollow bole of one of the massive trunks. For a tiny plant was perched there—alone on the edge in persistent growth—and sprouting from its leafy branches was a single swaying blossom—the rare and sacred Rose of Exumanities.

The bold little mouse steered himself closer to the wondrous bloom as best he could and within a few moments he was near enough to view the magnificent Rose. What he discovered there was the very strangest of all flowers, no greater in size than himself, but upon which each delicate petal contained the composite structure and living essence of each of the multi-worlds

which exist throughout all the netherspheres of time and space—within the minds of men and mice. Here was a key to all destinations within and without the universe—and of all the many thousands upon thousands of petals that instantaneously grew, blossomed, and withered away with the passing moments—there was but one which our tiny mouse must choose for the magical contrivances of Yabool-Syn.

"Choose correctly, Good Mouse!" were the words that somehow entered his mind from some faraway reality.

Our mouse was quite confused by this time and growing rather upset after viewing what was transpiring within the folds of some of those blossoming petals. Worlds and ways so unlike anything ever imagined intruded their harsh existence upon his reeling senses, causing a warping and distortion of all the realities of mice and men with which he was familiar.

"And of them all —which petal do I choose?" the mouse thought nervously to himself. For a frantic moment he had thought of making off with the entire Rose itself—but he somehow instinctively knew that this was something not allowed and impossible to accomplish—being far beyond the insignificant powers of one tiny mouse. No, he must choose only one petal and then quickly depart—trusting that he had chosen correctly and in the magical skills and promises of Yabool-Syn to bring him safely through the dimensional block and back to his own very-much-missed reality.

"Which petal do I choose?" our noble mouse called out to the nothingness that swirled about him in ever-increasing frequency—but there was no answer that issued forth from there, nor from that faraway room where Yabool-Syn pondered and paced so impatiently—so our brave mouse realized that for better or worse the decision was his—and his alone.

Once more the tiny mouse watched in stunned disbelief at all the multi-tiered realities that burst forth upon the petals of the Rose—some showing worlds quite rational and understandable, and others so bizarre and senseless that the very viewing of them caused him severe distress. How does one choose? What should he do? He wondered if he should choose a pastoral and known reality or perhaps the most wild and bizarre of them all! Or just perhaps something that was in between—something that looked interesting and yet not overly dangerous. Perhaps he should just close his tiny eyes and extract a fore claw to grab whichever petal first came into his grasp?

And what of Yabool-Syn and his labyrinthine magicks? What would the addition of a rare petal from this powerful Rose do to his shadow-purposed contrivements and poultices? And which petal? Might not one petal cause success and another much more dire consequences? Perhaps, but none of that was within the scope of a tiny mouse to decide, even one that had lately been exalted above all others of his kind by the administration of a potion whose wondrous effects were already wearing thin and would soon not

even be a memory in his dim rodent brain.

So our mouse made his valiant choice, and his tiny claws clutched up the sacred petal—but as he did so his mind once more plunged into that morass of dark and purposeless expectation which is the one singular reality of mice everywhere—and the reason for this most purposeful of choices was lost to him forever.

# PART THREE
## THE ROSE OF EXUMANITIES

Once more the hairs atop that worried old head turned gray as Yabool-Syn waited with wild impatience and hungry anticipation for his tiny messenger to return from the domains of mysterious Topaz. What seemed to flow by with the abandon of many days in his sphere of time and dance actually occurred in mere hours to the tiny mouse that suddenly appeared, carrying a gorgeous single rose petal delicately between loosened jaws.

"My Rose! My Rose!" Yabool-Syn cried and clapped his hands in utter delight, as he quickly grabbed the started creature into his eager grasp. With delicate long fingers the master mage prodded open the confused rodent's jaws and carefully extracted the precious flower petal—which did not so much as have a single tooth mark upon it's surface to mar its wondrous features and effects.

Yabool-Syn carefully set the mouse away within his cage, saying, "You have been a fine surrogate, my little fellow. Now away with you, while I direct my energies to more important matters."

Then Yabool-Syn gathered himself about the sacred petal and stared deeply into its folds and depths to become momentarily lost with what was occurring therein. And what he saw caused his features to ice over with an all-encompassing chill, as if the very flesh and bones of his being were now only a substance of frozen nothingness, lost upon a time field that does not exist, and blown upon the winds that go from Nothing to Nowhere. For the arch-mage of long forgotten Shenumbra now looked into the deep dark heart of Nothing—absolute, unreal, unfathomable Nothing—that which can not exist as any part of reality or in any reality at all. And yet, it is a Nothing that did somehow exist.

"This can not be!" Yabool-Syn shouted down into the glassy sphere of the petal of Exumanities. "Nothingness, by its very nature can not exist! Only something with substance and form and purpose can exist—that which is not real can *not* be real! That which is Nothing can *not* be something!"

And then the petal laughed—and Yabool-Syn shivered as he heard that terrible voice and watched in rapt fascination as it was borne upon the air by a sudden strong wind and deposited into a small vat of ill-smelling chemical mixtures and contrivances.

Upon impact from the petal there began a glowing and smoking and crying out of tearful pleas and dark warnings from the cauldron. And as the various elements continued their mixing, in a long lost alchemical process which produced a dangerous conundrum

known by some as The Elixir of Life—Yabool-Syn quickly opened *The Scarlet Book of Mages* and began a desperate search for that non-existent page which ancient legend says is not to be read by the eyes of men. Furiously the mage's fingers flowed through the book as nervous eyes scanned the bubbling, boiling mixture that was sending forth such a smoky stench throughout the building. He knew he must find that page—and finally stopped when he came to what was an apparently blank place in the book—unlabeled and unmarked, a mysterious unpainted sheet that had been magically inserted as a part of *The Scarlet Book of Mages*.

For this particular appearance of the magical page, it had caused itself to be located in the space between page 200 and 201—between the *Curse of Prognostic Digression* and *The Diminutive Scorn*. Here the blank sheet of paper suddenly came alive to host thousands of cursive letters that instantly began dancing around the page to eventually form into a message with significant meaning. And Yabool-Syn, full of fear and fascination began to read and read, and read furthermore what was written so mysteriously therein.

At the top of the page, in a deep and cursive script was titled, "The Retraction Principle, or Sliding Backwards Fearlessly"—and Yabool-Syn steeled his nerves and read quickly as the bubbling runaway elixir sparked and fumed and hissed into ghastly readiness at the other end of the room.

Yabool-Syn read, and in doing so he tried to under-

stand, but his fear and confusion took their mark upon his psyche and he was unsure of exactly what source to take regarding his runaway potion and whether the addition of Nothingness to Eternity would have any effect or use to him. Or would such a union unleash a dangerous monster that might destroy everything forever? Including his most precious self!

The mage quickly picked up yonder brave rodent messenger from the small cage where he had placed him a few moments before.

"You are needed once more, Good Mouse," Yabool-Syn cried as the terror welling within him fought to overwhelm his senses—the terrible fear that he might have lost all control over his bizarre creation—that he had, in fact, created something that might be dark and evil and hungry forever. With himself as the first victim!

The master mage feared that it was of paramount importance now to experiment with this dubious dark potion upon some insignificant surrogate first, so as to test its qualities. He could never be truly assured of safe results should he decide to avail himself of its promised boon of sacred Foreverness without a test.

"Good mouse, you are called to action once more!" Yabool-Syn said as he held the tiny creature in careful hands and moved closer to the horrible brew that sat spewing forth all manner of sparks and angry dark smoke from the cauldron. "You shall have the first taste. For your past favor to me—you shall now receive your vaulted reward. There is none better, Good Mouse,

than the gift of Foreverness—even under these dubious circumstances. You shall truly be a mouse among mice hereafter!"

The tiny mouse had other thoughts upon the matter but was held tightly and was unable to do anything but comply with his controller.

Then trying to stifle his cruel laughter, Yabool-Syn donned a pair of heavy protective gloves and a protective face mask, and with delicate care inserted a small eyedropper into that horrible bubbling mass of sparks and angry liquid to extract a few precious drops of the terrible potion.

"And now, little mouse," Yabool-Syn began, as he placed the instrument into the tiny mouth, he released a few drops down the rodent's throat, "be good and quiet and taste that of which the poets dream. Taste Foreverness!—and tell me if it be a good or bad thing to partake of."

# PART FOUR
## THE ELIXIR OF LIFE

Well, our little mouse soon began to show catastrophic effects from the potion which caused Yabool-Syn no end of concern and fear—concern and fear for himself of course—not for our little friend, Sir Mouse.

"See how his tiny body shakes and convulses, how the miniscule limbs grow rigid and the eyes red and large and cold." Yabool-Syn mumbled nervously as he paid careful attention to his surrogate messenger. He watched with dread at how the puny creature stirred and twisted and then ran mindlessly around the cage again and again and again, to finally collapse and fall to the floor motionless and apparently lifeless. It appeared an unintentional reaction and boded only ill for the promise the potion offered—and dashed all the master mage's plans into abject failure and alarm. For now he was not foolish enough to try the vile brew after what he had just seen take place. Now he must find some safe manner to dispose of this vile potion—which was not only useless to his plans—but posed a potential danger to himself as well should the dangerous contents of the potion decide to animate into some uncontrollable

monster.

"Foreverness…," Yabool-Syn said with a longing sadness, and there were actual tears dripping down the furrows of his old long face. "It is something I shall not be tasting—and meanwhile I have yon foul mixture, created after so much damnable work and peril— which I fear must now be destroyed before it destroys me."

The mage of Shenumbra then began a series of enchanted magic's and mystic incantations the likes of which had not been seen since the world's creation to bring forth from the dust and clay a gruesome golem in the gargoyle form.

The thing slowly formed up from the dust and dietrus of the surrounding area, muck and sludge left-over from a million rotting graves and disinterred bone matter. The tiny specks became alive with a motion all their own, came together at the mage's direction and began to form before his eyes into a truly terrible visage from the pit of darkness.

"You shall drink of Foreverness and Nothingness, oh ugly and vile beastly gargoyle, and be the vessel that holds it firm throughout time," Yabool-Syn commanded as the huge, horned monster flapped leathery wings and extended gruesome talons, working its jaws with precise hunger. It's clawed feet caused it to move forward as the thing approached the terrible elixir and picked up the bubbling cauldron with stone-hard claws.

"Now drink!" Yabool-Syn commanded the creature.

"Drink it all and drink it deep, you ugly monster—and you shall discover Nothingness and Foreverness—and eons hence when my time of life lapses you shall be recalled and resurrected to guard the scared crypt of Earth's greatest mage—in this last and greatest of its cities."

Then after drinking down the entire vile mixture the master mage caused the monster— that he had given the name of the Gargoyle of Crypts—to quickly vanish. Now Yabool-Syn once more turned his attention to the lifeless little mouse laying so quietly upon a leaf of lettuce in his lonely cage.

"Foreverness seems not to be such a desirable commodity as I had once thought, Little Mouse. Better to feed it to some ugly monster and begone with it than take any chances with my own precious persona," Yabool-Syn said in a salient whisper. "It seems, all things considered, that my little foray into these magical precincts has become a rather unsuccessful venture."

"I think not, Master Mage," a tiny voice surprisingly resounded within the old magician's head. The words were soft and lowly, the tone quiet and non-threatening, but strong in character nevertheless. It came from the tiny mouse, which was now beginning to stir and sit up on hind legs, eyes looking full into the face of Shenumbra's greatest sorcerer.

"Little Mouse?" Yabool-Syn stammered in evident surprise, "You are well? Alive? Then…there are no ill effects from the elixir?"

"None, Master Mage," the mouse replied with a toothy smile and a serious twitching of his small nose. "As you can see the elixir has restored the artificial enhancement of my intelligence, as well as conferring upon me the immortal gift of Foreverness."

"I see that only too well now, Sir Mouse." Yabool-Syn replied with his anger now warming as he realized his impatience and fear had caused a most injudicious loss of a most valuable and irreplaceable elixir. "And furthermore, I see that you have tricked me as well, with your choice of petal from the Rose."

"It was all for the good, My Lord Magician," the mouse responded fearlessly with a sharp stare into the cold orbs of the wizard. "Had you sampled the elixir the consequences to your person would have been dire and tragic—but for a tiny and insignificant mouse such as I—the effects proved negligible and the virtues many. For now I am also imbued with all manner of talismanic and necromantic lore, as well as possessed of vast reserves of preternatural strength and power, which can now be combined in many interesting ways with my new found knowledge."

Yabool-Syn rubbed his whiskered chin thoughtfully as he mulled over what the tiny creature before him was saying. He grew concerned. This little mouse could prove more trouble than he was worth and the arch-mage did not like what he was hearing—such bold and impudent words from a former messenger and servant did not have a pleasant ring in the mage's ears at all. Did this miniscule rodent now deem himself an

equal, a competitor—or more—to the great mage of Shenumbra? Yabool-Syn thought carefully upon this turn of events for he knew that where magic ruled far stranger things than this have happened and that he would have to tread lightly in his dealings with this tiny mouseling.

"I warn you, Sir Mouse, not to seek hegemony over Yabool-Syn—who is your rightful lord and master. Whatever your new gifts and talents, it is best to keep them unused and to yourself, rather than cause concern among myself and others of similar interests. Be wise, know your limits and do not interfere with your betters."

The mouse smiled with a delightful twinkling of the eyes and a twist of his long thin tail. "I did not ask for your gifts, Sorcerer, neither the former, nor the latter ones."

"That may be true," Yabool-Syn responded with a slight nod of acknowledgement, but his mind was already at work manufacturing scenarios of just what mischief and missions he could use such an interesting creature. Nevertheless, this mouse did present a serious potential danger to him as well, so he would have to gauge his intentions. Yabool-Syn did not like to dwell upon certain realities—for he knew that magicians of equal power and steeped in the same dark lore, when at war with each other, tend to cancel out the existence of one another. That was unacceptable. It was a sobering thought, and boded much caution on his part, for the master mage was not such a fool as to be misled by

the mere outward form of the tiny creature that stood before him. That what appeared to be one tiny mouse, now housed a powerful being of devastating potential and unknown direction. "And now, Sir Mouse, I must ask you in all frankness. What are your desires and your plans? I warn you that revenge taken against me can be a double-edged sword that will surely bring misery to the giver as well as the recipient."

The barest flicker of a grin came over the face of the little mouse.

"How wise you are—for a man, Master Mage," the tiny mouse replied with a darting grin.

"We gain what we can, day by day, Sir Mouse," Yabool-Syn answered with a mild shrug of heavy shoulders. He carefully watched the animal's bright eyes and the twitching tail that moved back and forth now so furiously as the mouse constantly sniffed the air currents surrounding him.

"However, Master Mage, I must tell you in all truthfulness that revenge, nor anger, are in my present repertoire," the mouse began, much to the magician's relief. "Rather more, now that I have this great intellect you have so dubiously presented upon me, I can remember much of what was forgotten upon my hasty return from the domains of Topaz."

"I see. And that was…?" Yabool-Syn prompted with renewed interest.

"That there are many thousands of petals which make up The Rose of Exumanities and that one of them contains the essence of an entire world of mice

such as I. Imagine the implications, if you will, Master Mage—an entire world where mice are as men and men—*are not!"*

"A world where mice rule and there are no humans at all? That is outrageous!"

"Not outrageous, Sorcerer, but rather, merely just wonderful! I shall harken there immediately."

"Sir Mouse!" Yabool-Syn demanded of the blasphemous rodent….

But the tiny mouse was already gone, floating in the dreams that make up Topaz—approaching a many-petaled blossom—and then making his own choice as to what he deemed the meaning of reality and then seeing to it that his dreams began to take shape and form and substance all around him.

\* \* \* \* \* \* \*

Deeply ensconced within the magician's lonely manse of cold stone, the master of arcane apothecary and all manner of necromantic arts recalled to life a hideous golem from the foul clay and dust of his surroundings.

It was with little joy that the master magician stood so still and crestfallen as he looked upon the grim visage of that most hideous monster, the Gargoyle of Crypts, that he had caused to now stand before him. The two regarded each other coldly.

"To be bested, and bested no less by a mouse of all the lowly creatures of creation is just too much! How can any magician live down such shame and insult—

how can any magician continue in the light of such knowledge!"

Yabool-Syn sighed heavily, a deep, dark tiredness had lately overcome him and he needed no talismanic auguries or charms to foretell that his allotted time on this sphere of existence had now run its course and it was his moment when the Great Dark of Death was fast approaching.

"Oh you gruesome gargoyle, you who stand there quietly and leer at me in such wicked fascination. Now it is time for you to take up your eternal vigil at the entrance to my death crypt, as sacred purpose fills the empty void between Foreverness and Nothingness until your own very last days. In such privileged manner shall you serve me until that last moment when Foreverness itself runs into the eternal dark of Nothingness."

The Gargoyle of Crypts waited....

# THE GARGOYLE
# OF CRYPTS

It was upon the outcroppings of Sheumbra—that last city of the planet Earth before the Great Dark rushed in to devour the world—where the hall of Oldearth's dead lay in musty, time-weathered pride.

Overlooking the wondrous manse, atop its pinnacled glory, stood the ever silent guardian—the Gargoyle of Crypts. Its eyes glared downward in ferocious fascination and ever watchful anticipation for any who might be so reckless as to enter the hallowed precincts of the crypts where lay the last of Earth's dead.

The ruins of Shenumbra, time-worn by wind and rain, crumbling from a once vast majesty, yet standing almost as in their ancient bygone glory, now lay forever mute. No longer did the once proud towers and minaret's enjoy the sweet trill of human laugher, or the tree-lined avenues and byways feel the soft tread of eager human feet moving so quickly about their all-important business.

Shenumbra now stood in disuse and decay, while the corpse-strewn passages that wound throughout the Hall of The Dead fell into ruinous destruction. Only

the Gargoyle of Crypts stood its ever silent watch over the remains of the dead throughout eternity.

That is what the star-traveling Leinites found when they came upon the planet and began to explore the ruins. With cries of voracious greed at their fabulous discovery, they began to systematically strip the remains of once-glorious Shenumbra like vultures attacking the dregs of a corpse.

It was not long before two of their number, one called Athubra, and the other known by the name of Throsis, came upon the ruinous precincts that made up the hall where so many of the dead had been entombed.

Athubra, one immersed in dark arts and forbidden knowledge, could scarce restrain himself at the mysteries that surely must lie within those deep and moldy chambers. With his companion, he forced open the great steel doors that led ever downward into the forbidden crypts, as with greedy anticipation both Leinites passed through the portal and into the antiquarian manse.

Upon careful but hasty examination, Athubra realized that buried with all these dusty dead old Earthers were many of the forbidden secrets of this long dead race. He marveled at bodies in perfect states of preservation, standing in stasis like grim stone statues lining the maze-like corridors that seemed to twist and turn interminably deeper and deeper into the gigantic structure. He noticed alien and mysterious cabalistic sign and sigils that seemed to hint at some dark sinister meanings; while his confederate, Throisis, called his

attention to a chamber he had found whose walls were lined from floor to ceiling with shelves full of strange and ancient tomes.

"We have made a great find here, Throsis!" Athubra rejoiced as he eyed the volumes and anticipated the wealth of knowledge that surely must be stored within them. "You must go back to the ship and bring all the others. Talk to old Abagutha. Tell him of these wondrous finds and of the knowledge and power which surely must be secreted here. Have him bring with him all the others, together with cases and other hardware, for the investigation and transportation of all that we have discovered."

Throsis acknowledged the order of his superior and was soon off upon his mission, the sound of his foot-falls diminishing as he moved farther away up the corridor.

All was quiet now, the ultimate silence of death surrounded the Leinite as he more closely examined the wonders surrounding him in that dank, dark chamber.

A gleam of intense satisfaction coursed throughout Athubra now that he had sent away his only competitor—for now the lost knowledge of this old dead world would be his alone. And once Throsis returned with the others, wily Athubra would be long in hiding with his treasures, learning their dark and forbidden secrets, and then through the use of certain spells and inducements, he planned to murder his companions. Then this great treasure would be all his to bring back to his home world, to study and use in his scheme to

gain power in the hierarchy of the Leinite world.

Knowing something of the talmaturgic arts, Athubra called forth to the ancient tomes that lined the walls of that dank chamber around him, and through a series of strange words and even more bizarre magical gestures, bade the volumes to come to life, to arise and to follow his instruction. Then in a mysterious and grotesque procession, the books suddenly lifted themselves off the shelves apparently of their own volition, floating with sinister movement through the air, following Athubra as he walked in front of them leading them into the corridor to find a suitable place for their concealment.

It was not long before he found a chamber that would meet his needs. Then giving a final order to the hoary texts, he watched with delight as they obediently hovered past him to enter the room, setting themselves down into neat little piles upon the cold tiles of the floor.

"Oh, obedient servants!" Athubra crooned in delight, "it will be through you that I shall unlock the dark wisdom and hidden secrets of these long dead ancients."

Sitting himself down comfortably, Athubra picked up one of the books at random and set it down to hover in the air before him.

"I now order you to speak to me of your knowledge," he commanded in a rasping voice, unable to withhold the excitement that had overcome him now—the excitement of the desecrator and grave robber.

At first there was no apparent result to his magical

directive, but then, ever so slowly, the musty cover of one of the ancient texts mysteriously began to open as if by an unseen hand. Upon the first page Athubra could see that complicated characters were inscrolled in some unknown language.

"Speak to me, demon, in a tongue I may comprehend!" Athubra ordered in haughty grandeur.

In a low voice that sounded like the rustling of wind through gravestones, Athubra heard strange haunting words that began forming inside his head.

*Beware the Gargoyle of Crypts*...he heard the phrase uttered in a sibilant whisper from the deep and dark nether regions of some faraway hell.

"Continue!" Athubra demanded in rapt fascination and eagerness as his voice own voice now cried out with insane delight and anticipation.

The frantic Leinite watched intently as unseen hands turned the page of the book before him, to reveal yet another page crammed full of the strange script.

Once again there was a sound as of rustling wind, even though that chamber lay secure from any currents of the outside air. And once again Athubra heard the low howling and whispered utterances of the captive voice within his head as it continue to speak.

*The Gargoyle of Crypts is the guardian of all the dead....*

Athubra suddenly startled.

He heard an unknown noise coming towards him from the corridor outside his chamber. It sounded like the shambling of feet. It must be Throsis and the others

returning. But so soon? If so, he would make quick work of them, but not yet. It would take them time to find him here. So he would not answer their pleas, and they would miss him in their search, for he was not ready to deal with them quite yet. But soon he would do so, once he had devoured the knowledge from these ancient texts.

Quickly the Leinite dabbled with a minor magical spell that would mask the chamber door and bar it from the entrance of his companions.

*...it roams these old halls seeking any who would disturb the eternal sleep of the dead*...the voice in his head intoned.

Again Athubra heard the noise. It was getting closer, and now that he heard it more clearly, he realized that it could not have been made by Throsis or any of the others.

*...the Gargoyle of Crypts was created ages ago by the living to watch over the dead, created in Foreverness by master mage Yabool-Syn. After a time something within the creature began to change of its own volition. It began to desire living victims to add to its empire of the dead. It took them all, the living and the dead as one into the crypts of death. The once great city of Shenumbra and its many people....*

Athubra darted a look toward the book with pained annoyance as he once again heard the strange sound drawing closer to his hiding place.

*The Gargoyle of Crypts....*

"Be quiet!" Athubra commanded. "Stop your words

now! I do not want to be found out!"

The unnatural winds increased, and the small chamber grew cold as the softness of the demonic voice now grew harsh and loud.

*Thou hast commanded me to speak, thy may not stop thine words until the entire story be told!*

"I command you to be quiet, damned demon!" Athubra shouted in anger, for he heard the noise now coming closer and it seemed to be just without his chamber. The sound of it, the feel of what might be there, sent cold shivers of fear though the Leinite as he tried to focus his powers to see what was beyond the door. It was a useless effort, for he realized some greater strength of magic now overpowered his own.

*The Gargoyle of Crypts comes for all of those who....*

"Be silent, demon!" Athubra cried at the book that lay open before him, as he suddenly turned towards the doorway in sheer terror. For now he heard a frenzied pounding of something outside, something of great power seeking entrance.

Terrified by what lay beyond that portal, Athubra focused his powers in a vain effort to ensure his spell upon the door would hold. However, he knew that it was only a simple portent and not one of any real power.

*...to add you to the legions of the dead, to be collected and watched throughout all the bleak, dark eternities....*

"No!" Athubra shouted.

*It awaits. It is for you now!* the hideous demon-

spawned voice mocked, the words reverberated through Athubra's mind, haunting him to the depths of his very soul.

"No!" Athubra cried out. "It can not be!"

Fierce sounds came to his ears from the outside corridor until he saw the door shake with one mighty convulsive heave to fall to the floor before him with a resounding whack. When the dust cleared, the wily Leinite saw framed there in the opening a monstrosity born of out the deepest and darkest of nightmares. Silently the hideous creature advanced towards the terror-stricken Leinite....

\* \* \* \* \* \* \*

Throsis, old Abagutha, and a small party of the crew entered the musty maze that was the hall of Oldearth's dead. For a long time they searched for their companion, Athubra, until Throsis, calling the others to him, had finally found his master.

Frozen in a death-like visage of terror, yet perfectly preserved like some statuesque museum piece carved out of living flesh, Throsis and the others looked piteously upon their lost companion. It was their companion's visage that unnerved them the most, the look of abject fear was encompassed within a veil of such utter sadness that it brought tears to many of their eyes. Saddened by what they saw in their companion's stark face, the Leinites could hardly look into the deep pools in his eyes, horrible dark pits that seemed to silently cry out with all the suffering and torment of the truly

damned.

Surrounding the body, the Leinites noticed that the floor was scattered with many piles of ancient books belonging to the dead of this dead world. Once such volume lay open held motionless in the air as if by invisible hands before Athubra's frozen form.

"This is most strange," Throsis said.

"It is demon-spawned leavings," another said.

The Leinties stared at the floating book with fear and shock.

*...the Gargoyle of Crypts guards its treasures most jealously from all...*a soft sibilant voice intoned from an unknown location.

Throsis and the others startled. None of them had whispered the eerie words. In wide-eyed terror they realized the words had been spoken into their minds, and they now looked upon the book floating in the air before them with fear as one page slowly turned, as if by some unseen hand.

The Leinites began to show their alarm, but bravely they tried to master their shaken emotions. They were, after all, logical star-faring beings. They began to collect the books and box them up for transport—all except the one hanging magically in the air before them. "Leave that one," the leader ordered. "Do not even touch it."

The others did as their leader ordered. Nevertheless all their senses sharpened, as did their suspicions.

"Do you hear something?" old Abagutha asked tensely. He was trying to hold back his fear in a valiant

attempt that was proving more unsuccessful as each tense moment passed He stared at the mysterious book hanging there in the air before him, as did all the others. It was impossible…magic…evil…worse…. What?

Throsis, who was accounted by all to have the best hearing, bent his head to give a listen.

"It is nothing, just the rustling of the winds in the corridor without," Throsis said hopefully, in a vain effort to calm his companions, and himself.

"There be no winds in this chamber, within or without," one of the small party of Leinites ventured nervously.

"Well, whatever it is," Abagutha said in a doom-laden voice, "it seems to be coming closer."

Once more the rustling of ill winds sounded, this time accompanied by a mysterious voice howling in delicious torment, so horrendous to hear that it turned warm Leinite blood to a chill thin liquid in the veins of all who heard it.

"It is a demon!" A Leinite screamed out in full panic now.

"Yes, surely a demon!" one shouted shaken to his core.

"Let us leave this terrible place at once!" Another cried out in open fear. "Let us leave before it is too late for us—as it was too late for poor Athubra!"

With the speed of cold sharp fear, Throsis and the others quickly packed up what they could and quickly left the dark chambers in a headlong rush to reach their ship. Hastily they entered the vessel and prepared to

leave this world of horrors.

"We will be ready to depart in a few moments," old Abagutha said to his crew. And though they were now safely ensconced within their vessel his impatience was goaded by the numbing fear that held sway over them all. Would they be able to get away before it was too late?

"It will be soon," Throsis told himself and those around him. "We will be free and home soon!" He was consciously trying to restrain the fear that had but moments ago taken control of his being. He had almost achieved his aim when both he and his companions were alerted by a sound that was coming from outside their vessel.

It was an eerie sound, as though a mighty pounding was somehow continually being repeated upon the outer hull of the ship. But what?

"By my ancestors! What can that sound be?" the Leinite leader said trying to hold down his panic as he readied the ship for launching.

Throsis shook nervously, "I do not know and I do not want to find out. I suggest we lift-off immediately and get as far away from this world as we can before it is too late."

His words were hardly spoken when Abagutha prayerfully depressed the firing mechanism which sent the Leinite spaceship into the cold dark of the ancient night sky.

"It is done," Abagutha told those around him in relief as the ship already headed into the planet's outer

atmosphere.

"And not soon enough for me," Throsis added as he wiped the sweat from his face and looked around at his nervous companions, each of which felt they had escaped from some deadly evil they did not even want to contemplate.

"Soon we shall be home," Abagutha told his team and just the sound of his optimistic words seemed to relieve their—and his own—terrible fear and tension. "Let us open the viewport so that we can gaze upon the star field. The Leinite world will come into view soon and it will do us all good to see home after being on this thrice-damned world."

"A good suggestion," Throsis replied with a smile. Silently he pressed the control switch that slowly opened the huge metal plates which covered the view-port before them.

Throsis could not mouth one word at what he now saw.

For there before him—surrounded by the lonely blackness of infinite space, peering with malevolent gaze and hunger into the ship's tiny control room— was a monster born out of the most foul nightmares imaginable—the Gargoyle of Crypts!

# THE LIGHT OF DARKNESS

# PART ONE
## THE LEINITE SHIP

The ship phased into real-time within the blink of an eye, the automatics causing it to hover in the rainbow red sky, obstructed by the planet's numerous suns, moons and cottony swirls of cloud stuff.

It was a ship of death, a lifeless hulk of lost space debris, a mystery to the Leinite leaders who appointed Onman Quay to the dubious duty of investigatory analyzer and reporter.

"You have until the red moon sets, Quay," said Chief Interpolator Barazza, with a massive scruff of brows and twitch of whiskery jowls. His eyes shone bright red, and his temple horns shone with sharp ivory whiteness, the tips capped in the latest style with twists of filigree gold with inlaid silver.

"I hear and shall obey, Leinite leader," Quay responded with a furl of cape, to be off with usual Leinite immediateness upon this most important of missions.

He reached the luckless ship in short order, entering it where it hovered in polite and lonely planetary orbit, and soon began the lengthy process of examination.

He did not find a sign of life anywhere within the huge interplanetary vessel, nor could he find any clue, device, or hinting signal as to what had happened to his Leinite brethren.

With a quiet shrug he seated himself in the captain's console, his sense of immediateness stymied by the sudden perplexities of this bizarre case. Brethren do not just disappear!

"There were over five hundred of our people on this ship! Abagutha, and many other friends of ours were lost. But where?" Quay spoke to the open air with a feeling of imponderable weight settling upon his shoulders with each successive moment. "What has happened here? How am I to find answers when I do not even know the questions themselves that must be asked?"

"Each of the brethren knows that simple answer, Master Quay," came a tiny muffled voice from deep within his pocket pouch.

Quay had all but forgotten about Talsheen, the tiny Torva, a furry rodent-like being that was his psychical symbiotic companion and partner in the investigatory process. He deftly withdrew the small animal and placed him on the arm of the chair beside him.

"We have a problem here, Talsheen. One of inexplicable proportions, and obviously dire consequences. Five hundred brethren do not just disappear—and if so, how did they disappear so that there is no sign of them whatsoever? The Chief Interpolator and the Leinite Council themselves are substantially concerned with

this matter."

"Undoubtedly so, Master Quay," Talsheen responded with a flitting of tongue and ears. "Is this not the research vessel that was sent into the Hot Region at the galactic core?"

"Yes, a lengthy mission, planned to visit a multitude of worlds. And who knows what was found out there. We have until the red moon sets to find the answer, otherwise the vessel will be towed into deep space and annihilated into its basic molecular components."

A fit ending for such a luckless ship," Talsheen replied.

"Perhaps, but it leaves us with a telling question, Talsheen, one that haunts me as much as it must haunt this great empty vessel itself. What has happened to the crew?"

"Then we shall have to investigate," Talsheen added with a quipping of his long furry ears. Quay knew the gesture as the beginnings of the creature's use of their psychical symbiosis, as its thoughts now ranged over the entire vessel, searching, examining, hunting for tastes and flavors of what had happened.

"For what exactly?" Talsheen questioned.

"For any manner of clue, Talsheen," Quay said thoughtfully. "Have you sensed anything regarding the lost ones?"

"There is a curious and violent residue that lingers within the structure. It has eaten deeply into the very metal of the vessel itself. And yet, what has happened to the five hundred perplexes me—it is as if they were

swallowed into the deep pool of time and space itself. I fear, Master Quay, that they are lost to us forever, deitrus to be blown upon the eternal winds of some far away world."

"Quite poetic nomenclature, especially for a Torva, Talsheen, but words that only continue our own obvious obfuscation of this implacable predicament."

"A pretty speech yourself, Master Quay, and a laude your use of language, but it in itself gets us nowhere as well," Talsheen quilled his nose tip with an almost delicate flurry of rapidity.

Quay watched in silence as the little Torva flexed his tiny nose tip, desperately seeking resonance of whatever residue of past experience remained within the mysterious vessel. His fury ears quipped tightly, roving for sounds inaudible even to the delicate Leinite ear, sounds lost within a saraband of time, eternity's last age-old recordings of past events, anything that might give some hint as to what had occurred upon this luckless vessel.

Finally Talsheen slumped into a crumpled heap of tiredness and Quay, picking him up with delicate and loving fingers, placed him within the bow of his arm. And much as one does with a tiny baby, Quay slowly rubbed the soft fur in the deep swirling patterns that Torvas enjoyed so much after the deep exhaustive shock of psychic evaluation.

"Ah, Master Quay," Talsheen responded with an awakening smile. He stretched, shook his head, and then said, "I believe this case presents hitherfore

unforeseen difficulties of a serious nature we have never encountered before."

"Please explain?" Quay asked, rubbing the tiny creature's fur with renewed interest, and then slowing his actions down when he realized that his own active impatience threatened to de-fur the Torva there. "What exactly have you discovered?"

"Nothing concrete, Master Quay. But there is a foreign presence strongly felt in the past life experience of this vessel and the members of the crew. It is a most malign and fearfully dangerous creature—some kind of terrible monster created out of the worst of nightmares..."

Onman Quay was silent for a long moment, thinking over Talsheen's words with careful deliberation. The Torva was not often wrong on it's assumptions. Quay nodded, of course there had to be some manner of outside agency involved in all this, five hundred brethren do not just disappear without a trace. Talsheen's news was logical enough, but the words from his tiny Torva friend sent a shiver through Onman Quay nevertheless. Just what were they dealing with here?

"Then that settles it, Talsheen. There must be something aboard this vessel. Or, it *was* aboard! That is what we shall now determine as a certainty. We will call reinforcements and run a complete scan and search of this haunted vessel. And I do mean complete—down to the molecular level! If there is anything aboard—rest assured we will find it!

It was not long thereafter that the huge vessel was crawling with all manner of investigatory personnel, poking and probing and scanning with all manner of mysterious equipment and computational devices. Other aids were also utilized—First Degree Torvas from Lokinsee were brought in to form resonance rings, mutes and mindsayers and other sensitives from the faraway lands were also to be seen hard at work.

Hints were discovered, clues evolved from the darkness of obscurity, and all the while the information seemed to grow more and more threatening. Finally, Onman Quay and Talsheen hooked themselves into a multi-mind link with all the other investigators, as all their hints and clues, suppositions and theories flooded forth into their subconscious memory. The process was a rapid one and an exhausting one, but after a sufficient period of rest and reorientation, Onman Quay and Talsheen were ready to proceed anew upon their investigation.

To begin with, they departed the vessel. A thorough investigation had found nothing—or at least there was nothing presently onboard the huge ship that could answer any of their questions.

"We must look elsewhere, Talsheen," Quay said as they departed the vessel for the planetary surface below. "I make no bones about the concern that has gripped me, for it is now quite evident that the creature we seek is now loose upon our beloved world—somewhere—free at this very moment!"

"And engaged in what manner of terrible mischief?"

Talsheen continued the thought that was uppermost now in Quay's own mind. What, in fact, was this creature's location? And what was it doing here on the Leinite world?

The thought of such a dangerous monster loose upon the home world had Quay and the tiny Torva in the utmost alarm.

# PART TWO

## THE GARGOYLE'S INTENT

The Gargoyle of Crypts stepped lightly with insectoid precision, eyes scanning the area before it with a cold and dark hunger so stark and sharp that it's gaze seemed to shear the very molecules of the air before it into abject submission and terror. Here was a being totally alien to the soft soil and clear air of the Leinite world—here was a beastly thing from the depths of darkest nightmare—created to instill fear and terror at the mere sight of it. Here was the thing called the Gargoyle of Crypts.

The creature flew over the Leinite countryside, shearing the very air with its cold leathery wings, while eyes and ears scanned all directions in a seeking search pattern of dire purpose and dark intent.

Finally, the creature's attention was drawn to a large monument that sat upon a distant horizon of azure sky and a swirling overhead mass of moons and clouds. With an astonishingly angular change in its direction and speed, the gargoyle rushed its hurried flight in a direction toward this strange manifestation of other-worldly architecture.

It was not long before the gargoyle reached the massive monument, and found it to be a tremendous structure apparently sitting alone on the vast plains of the Leinite wilderness. But the creature surely recognized the mammoth monument for what it truly was—a massive mausoleum dedicated to the Leinite dead. In that way it was not at all unlike the ancient crypts of Shenumbra on the world known as Oldearth, whose dead he had been created to guard so long ago in those timeworn mystical ruins.

The Gargoyle of Crypts had found a purpose and a further reason for existence on this strange new world. It now approached the massive structure in ever closer investigatory flybys. Immediately the creature noticed a lofty pinnacle far above all others which it might utilize as an excellent guardian tower and perch. The gargoyle made rapid advancement through the thin Leinite atmosphere to this destination.

\* \* \* \* \* \* \*

Onman Quay and Talsheen were looking for a creature the likes of which no Leinite or Torva could ever imagine the existence of. All around the planet, in every facet of Leinite and Torva society, all were on the lookout for the strange nightmare-like creature that had come to their world. The military and civilian authorities actually headed up the search, but individual Leinites maintained a constant vigilance and watchfulness for anything that was out of the ordinary.

So when Onman Quay received a data message

relayed from Ardeen Continent, through the Central Terminal Nexus of Manquen, from a minor public official on the outskirts of Pleenash Farm, he didn't think much of it at first. But when his attention was drawn to Speaker Calman's words from the Pleenash Farm, things began to click when that worthy old gentleman mentioned he had spotted a "flying monster" headed in the direction of the Great Mausoleum at Qnash.

* * * * * * *

Qnash is the loneliest of areas, the home of an entire world's dead must be the loneliest place on that world. Leinites and Torvas alike dread the place and shun it, for the terrible stench of death and decay assail the very air of the region and spread out in strangling putrescence no matter wherever you go there. This is the place where the Leinites entomb all those who have expired throughout the vast history of the planet. This is Qnash—the Home of the Dead!

Onman Quay did not like the area, and his symbiotic friend liked it even less, but both had a mission to perform. Quay slowly brought his tiny flier toward the massive structure. It was as large as an entire city—encompassing many miles of underground tunnels, chambers, vaults, and necrotorium. Quay strained his eyes to see if he might spot anything out of the ordinary in the area.

"I do not like being here, Leinite," Talsheen said using the proper, strict form of speech to his friend, indicating a most serious and anger-fearful approach

of verbal communication used only in times of dire stress and imminent danger

"Talsheen, my friend, we have a duty," Onman Quay reminded with a smile as he banked the tiny flier around a massive western wall of a particularly high tower. "You are allowing imagination to run away with you. You do not even know what it is that we are looking for."

"You are so very correct, Leinite," Talsheen responded sharply. "And it is that very fact which is sending my tiny legs to clacking and my thin fingers to twitching."

"Well, hopefully, my little Torva friend, we will straighten this out soon enough." Then Onman Quay turned the flier in a wide arc backdropping to another direction of the tower that he'd not noticed before.

"Whatever is that, Leinite?" Talsheen asked in evident concern as his Leinite companion looked off to where the Torva was pointing.

"I am not sure, Torva," Onman Quay said a bit tensely himself now. His own nerves were growing taut and fearful and it was a real struggle to press ahead. He looked around him carefully. "I thought I saw something of interest back there, something that looked very much out of place, Talsheen."

There was a pause of silence for a moment as both investigators examined the surrounding area more closely.

"I think I see what you mean, Master Quay. If I can but draw your attention to yonder tower. I see atop its

lofty pinnacle what may very well be the answer to all our questions—and perhaps all our nightmares as well!"

Onman Quay brought the tiny flier up higher and closer to the building and then set it to hovering a short distance from the dark and silent thing that was perched so quietly atop the pinnacle of the highest tower. Onman Quay, in spite of himself, could only gasp a breath of cold fear and revulsion.

"My God of Gods!" was all that the Leinite could utter for a long moment, his tiny partner sat frozen in fear. Then in a stressful whisper he muttered, "That old Pleenash farmer was indeed correct, such a monster I have never seen on this side of life!"

"A truly terrible thing, fearful in extremis," Talsheen answered softly, ensconced in the safety of the crook of Quay's arm. The very appearance of the creature was having a malevolent effect upon the psyche of the tiny Torva "I think we should not forget the rest of the farmer's words. He described the creature as a 'flying monster'."

Onman Quay looked at the creature with renewed fear and alarm.

Finally Talsheen muttered, "I think it best that you immediately engage the armaments—such as we have in this miniscule vessel—and have them lock-on this monster for its immediate and total destruction."

Onman Quay could only nod and slowly did as Talsheen suggested, but he did it with a half-hearted somnambulant desire that caused the tiny Torva quite

a bit of curious consternation. Quay knew they were dealing with an apparently dangerous creature, one responsible for the death and disappearance of over five hundred Leinite brethren. That was a situation that neither Onman Quay nor Talsheen could take lightly. However the creature had shown no violence or acts of aggression at all.

And yet, as Quay watched the silent, immobile creature sitting there so alone—hunched up with knees into hoary chest, leathery black bat wings folded down into its' massive and ugly dark body—the investigatory analyzer could not help but become fascinated by it. For here was a totally alien creature, a form of life— or something life-like—from another world!

Onman Quay began asking himself a hundred wild and curious questions about the creature. Was it intelligent? Why was it here on the Leinite world? What kind of thing was it? And finally, was it possible to communicate with it? The idea fascinated him and he was determined to give it a try.

Talsheen, concerned about the delay, quietly moved up to Quay's shoulder and whispered into his ear with fierce determination, "Now is your chance! Destroy it quickly! Before it awakens and kills us both! Hurry now! Kill it, Leinite!"

"Enough, Torva!" Onman Quay said as he studied the horrible monster before him, transfixed by its truly horrid appearance, its repugnant ugliness and the dreadful look of doom and despair that it wore like the very face of death itself. Silently he wondered, what

manner of thing could this be?

"It is evil, Leinite! I am sure of it!" Talsheen murmured quietly to his friend, knowing somehow now that his cause was lost.

"It is alien, Torva. Whether it is evil or not is not for you or I to judge at present without further information."

"God of all Gods! Are you ill? Insane? This thing butchered five hundred of your brethren, Leinite!" Talsheen explained fearfully once again. "What is wrong with you? I believe you are somehow being extracted from yourself—becoming lost within the power of the thing."

Onman Quay only laughed at the ridiculousness of that statement, but he did it with a soft and malicious grinding of teeth that was most unusual and disconcerting for the Torva to see.

"There is great danger here, Leinite," Talsheen warned.

"Be silent!" Quay finally barked as his hand now left the weapon console and he began to maneuver the scout craft ever closer to the creature before them.

"What are you doing? Are you Mad?"

"I said: be silent, Torva!"

"You are becoming transfixed by the glamour of that diabolical beast! It's insidious evil power has cast a pall upon you that has blinded your thoughts and judgment, Leinite," Talsheen replied carefully. The tiny Torva moved closer to the weapons console—closer to the lock-on switch of the firing button—closer still as

the tiny creature used all his strength and energy to depress that small red button.

Instantly a lethal rocket was fired from the vessel—to cause a direct hit upon the alien creature.

At first, it appeared that the weapon was without any visible effect at all, and Talsheen muttered with nervous despair at the lack of any damage their terrible weapon had inflicted upon the monster.

Onman Quay could only shout with fearful anticipation as he noticed first one eye and then the other eye of the great beast—open and look at him. Those dreadful eyes gazed intently upon him and then Talsheen, with a malevolent red hatred that sent chills through both of them.

"God of all Gods! Can you still call that thing other than evil, Leinite? Please, Onman Quay, let us leave this creature to the Leinite dead. I have no more need nor desire to feed its terrible hunger or anger."

Onman Quay was finally roused out of his dark lethargy as if coming out of a dream. He looked into the deep red eyes of the Gargoyle of Crypts and a cold chill racked his features. "What manner of monster are you?"

And then, with an apparent deliberate slowness and insectoid precision, the gargoyle slowly moved its neck and shifted its icy gaze, the mouth opening to exhibit a long red tongue that flicked about in the air with a fierce reptilian implication. It was a terrible thing to view.

"Quick, Leinite, let us leave this place immediately!"

Talsheen replied quickly.

"No," Onman Quay replied brusquely. "We must not leave, we must defeat or destroy this monster. We can not allow it to roam the Leinite world at will."

"And how do you intend to stop it, Quay?" Talsheen added in relief that his companion had finally opened his eyes about the thing, but still felt a bitter scorn born out of intense fear.

"Through our Leinite and Torva powers—the symbiosis of our knowledge and abilities can defeat this monster—or at least render it impotent of danger to us. We must do it, Talsheen, otherwise our beloved world will be devoured by this creature and we will be helpless to prevent any of it."

"And so, Leinite, what is your plan? You wish to make the linkage once again?" Talsheen said, obviously quite terrified by the prospect as his small eyes stared into the dark creature before them—and as it stared back at him with a doomed intensity. It was a most disconcerting situation for the tiny Torva to find himself in.

"It appears a linkage is the only way, though it makes us vulnerable to any attack, it is our last chance, Talsheen."

Talsheen nodded dubiously, the fear surging through him despite the fact that he tried to put up a brave front.

Then Onman Quay brought the flier closer still to the ledge and put the automatics on hover. Talsheeen grew ever more fearful as he drew closer to the monster—as he was placed upon the right shoulder of his master—

as he and the Leinite made the mental linkage that made their minds as one.

Both were immediately startled by the amount of power inherent in that link, and the instantaneous psychical communication between the Leinite and Torva, which was resultant in such a tight bonding of the two.

Onman Quay whispered a short stanza from *Delirium Lament*, an ancient Torva prayer-song for lost causes and hopeless quests. Then Quay boldly opened the flier cockpit, and with Talsheen holding on tightly upon his shoulder, he precariously moved out onto the narrow ledge upon which the leering monster—the Gargoyle of Crypts—devoured them with red eyes of intense hatred.

"Alyeee!" Talsheen muttered in a fearful whisper as Quay reluctantly approached the fierce alien monster face to face.

The Gargoyle of Crypts did nothing. Amazingly, it did not attack. In fact, it did not move at all. It only stared at the Leinite and Torva interlopers with its usual fierce deliberation and insectoid frigidity— tongue finally flickering a bare yard from Quay's sweaty face—Talsheen by now was reduced to a quivering ball of furry fear.

"What are you?" Onman Quay asked through his Leinite-Torva linkage, not in actual words, but through mental images which he sent deep into that strata of existence within the mass of nothingness that opted for the mind of the monstrous gargoyle.

Not a single word was uttered in question, not a single word was issued in reply—but deep within that subconscious level of inner mind that functioned as the brain of the dreadful beast there was a dim glimmering of acknowledgement that shone dully—so very far away—in some extreme distance of never-ending space and time. And then Quay and the Torva bravely entered the inner workings of the terrible monster before them.

"Be careful, Master Quay, we are entering the creature's world now—it will be easy to become lost, misled, destroyed. Seek the light, but move with speed, for the longer we remain here the more our structure will become attuned to the creature's own structure. We run the risk of being compromised, of being absorbed if we are not watchful and quick."

"Then we proceed to the light, far off in yonder distance, Talsheen, and the faster we get there the faster we will have the answers to our questions."

Within the mind of the hell-creature, through countless corridors of hate, loathing rivers of blood-red fire, skies of outrage—and a vast all-encompassing darkness beyond the fields of time itself—there shone that faraway glimmer of light. To this point Onman Quay and Talsheen rushed, using it as a beacon for their hazardous quest. It was not long before the linkage of Leinite and Torva consciousness reached this secluded distant spot.

"The Spot of Life, Quay," Talsheen said in awe. "The area of creation. Look down deeply into it and see the

history of all that is the dark purpose of this horrible being."

Onman Quay moved closer to the Spot of Life. He found that his consciousness was now in a deep pit alive with swirling sides, a timeless malevolence, constant causal complications, an intense landscape where mystery and reality interchanged at will. It was chaos, unbound by law or any rational sense, or anything that a Leinite investigator or his tiny Torva companion might bare any relation to understanding. Yet, Onman Quay and Talsheen persisted in their journey, continuing their investigation as they continued to delve down into the deep mire of the creature's essence.

"We are there! Are you ready, Talsheen?" Quay asked his furry companion.

"No, Quay, I shall never be truly ready for what you now plan, but proceed. Proceed and be done quickly!"

And then Onman Quay, with his miniscule symbiotic companion holding on for dear life, suddenly jumped into the center of that swirling mass of hate and fear and dark torment that was the Spot of Life within the mind of the Gargoyle of Crypts.

Down, down, deep they fell. Turning and tossing as the sides of the funnel twisted and swirled around them in a cacophony of mixed images, blurred colors, bizarre sounds, and incoherent ideas and thoughts. It was a sweltering mass of confusion unlike anything imaginable. They were inside the dark soul of the monster, and the realization sent tremors of awe and fear through the two mind travelers and threatened to

break their sensitive linkage—which at that moment would have been a disaster for them. Meanwhile, there stood the empty physical bodies of Quay and Talsheen, silently before the vile monstrosity that held sway out upon the ledge in what passed for conscious reality—lifeless and empty shells now.

Yet within the creature all was a mass of confusion. Deeper still the two mind- travelers fell. They plunged ever deeper into the bottom of that horrible well, until they had reached the very bottom with a seemingly slow-motion descent to the well floor.

Here, was found relative calm, like the eye of some chaotic hurricane. Onman Quay and Talsheen, holding their linkage ever tighter than ever now and dear to their very lives, communicated instantaneously, each intercepting all the vast knowledge and past experiences of the creature swirling within the tempest before them.

Then finally, there it lay, the story of the creature that was known as the Gargoyle of Crypts—unfolding before them like the stripped petals of a great black rose. The horrible creation of the vile thing millions of years in the past by that arch-mage of Oldearth sorcerers, Yabool-Syn.

Next was shown the particular manner in which the monster took up its unique guardianship over the crypts of ancient Shenumbra and of Oldearth's dead. Still more time passed. Eventually, a Leinite starship landed upon the strange old world, and the story grew when greedy defilers ransacked the tattered libraries

and crypts for long-buried riches and forbidden lore. And lastly, there was the recreation of the events that occurred aboard the doomed Leinite ship—lost in the space lanes between the planets, with the horrible monster loose and aboard—a mass of terrible destruction and death-dealing doom that no Leinite mind would ever believe possible in its wildest nightmares.

"And now, Leinite?" Talsheen said with much more nervous reservation. "We know the story now. What are we to do about it? Destroy the monster? Can this monster even be destroyed?"

"Must it be destroyed, Talsheen?" Onman Quay countered thoughtfully, much to his tiny companion's discouragement. "The creature was designed and directed for one specific purpose, and that purpose is the guardianship of the dead. I see no reason why it could not stand guard over Leinite dead as it once did over the dead from some long ago forgotten planet called Oldearth."

"But, Quay…?"

"Let it be. As long as it stays at it's post and keeps it's purpose here, we may not have to destroy it. If, as you say, that is even possible. Which I doubt. In the meantime, we might use the time to devise an effective weapon for use against it, should it ever grow restive and decide to withdraw from it's duty here."

"Of course this monster will have to be watched every moment," Talsheen asked carefully, suspicious in the extreme.

"Without a doubt, that is of the utmost importance,"

Onman Quay responded to his friend. "And now my worthy Torva, let us leave here and return to the cleaner air of conscious reality. Break the linkage and let us withdraw to the reality of our own bodies back in the real world."

"And that is your best suggestion yet, Master Quay, for I grow weary and dirty down here, and seek home and comfort, and the bright light of the real world. Our world."

\* \* \* \* \* \* \*

The red moon had set, and the black moon was up high in the Leinite sky. Dark and invisible as usual.

Onman Quay, investigatory analyzer, along with Talsheen, his Torva companion and symbiote, had just finished making their report to the Leinite leaders. Immediately plans were in progress for the development of weapons to neutralize the invading monster should it seek to augment its realm of the dead with other living Leinite souls, or should it depart it's post of guardianship at Qnash and seek mobility over the Leinite world.

"In the meantime, Quay, the Council will see to it that the creature is constantly kept under watch. A team of specialists will keep a good eye on it, and who knows, perhaps we'll not even need the death weapons to be put to use against it after all. That would be good all around. The weapons would prove quite devastating to our world and our people as well as the creature. All in all, you accomplished your mission in all respects

but one, Quay," one of the council leaders told him.

"Sir?" Quay asked, and Talsheen's eyes perked up as well now.

"The five hundred brethren? Our Leinite brethren! What has become of them?" the leader asked with rapt consternation.

Onman Quay nodded slowly. "Deep space, Leinite Master. Our brethren left the spaceship in fear of their own volition. Even though they knew it meant certain death in the cold of unprotected deep space, they decided to face that certainty rather than face the fearful unknown that discovery of the gargoyle represented to them."

"So the monster did not murder them?"

"No, their fear caused their own demise," Quay replied sadly.

"I see, Quay. But do you feel that the monster would have murdered our brethren had they remained aboard with it?" the leader asked thoughtfully.

"That is a question I can not answer. All new contacts encompass a certain measure of danger and the unknown. This gargoyle adds fear and loathing into that substantial equation—that terrible search for the light—lost, alone, obscured by all surrounding darkness. It is an interesting question. One that I can not answer."

"It is a heady mixture that few are able to overcome," Talsheen said softly, adding, "as my own fearful behavior concerning the creature recently showed."

Onman Quay smiled and rubbed the soft fur that

grew in little round tufts around Talsheen's neck. The Torva loved the attention and trilled lightly with pleasure.

The mission was done and the results were satisfactory, so it was not long before the two companions left the massive chamber of the Leinite Council to take up their new residence, as well as begin another mission that had recently been offered to them.

* * * * * * *

The Great Mausoleum at Qnash stretched seemingly forever, drowned in the fiery suns of the Leinite world. Huge structures, honeycombed corridors, great dank catacombs and grim moldy mortuaries—a hundred leagues of the old and ancient dead—stretched in long lonely lines below the surface and attested to the singular nature of this silent city. It truly was the Kingdom of the Dead.

And there upon the highest pinnacle of the Great Mausoleum, atop its glorious summit, was a flat-ledged perch upon which sat a dark stony structure of black grain and hard gaze. With leathery wings folded back, hunched legs pulled tightly into its black chest, its red eyes scanned the surrounding area for a hundred leagues in all directions.

And at their new residence, overlooking the vast stony gaze of the thing known as the Gargoyle of Crypts, sat Onman Quay and his friend and companion, Talsheen, watching the gargoyle—as it sat on its perch and watched them.

And smiled..

Talsheen shivered from where he lay in the crook of Onman Quay's arm. "Master Quay, it is watching us, just as we watch it. I hope the day will never come when it decides to make a move and leave it's perch at Qnash."

Onman Quay nodded carefully, "I only hope we will be ready when—or if—it does, Talsheen."

# ABOUT THE AUTHOR

**GARY LOVISI** has been a fan of the works of fantasy fabulists H. P. Lovecraft, Clark Ashton Smith, and Jack Vance for decades. The three stories in this volume have been written in the style of Smith, with the addition of a substantial Vance influence. Lovisi is also a Mystery Writers of America Edgar Award nominee for his crime fiction, and a Western Writers of America Spur Award winner for his editing of *Hardboiled* magazine. He is also the editor of *Paperback Parade*, a book collectors magazine, and publishes various books under his Gryphon Books imprint. His latest books are *Ultra-Boiled* (Ramble House, 2010) a collection of twenty-three hard crime and noir stories, and *Bad Girls Need Love Too* (Krause Books, 2010), a celebration of sexy vintage paperback cover art. You can contact him or find out more at his website:

www.GryphonBooks.com